Parker opened the gate and led Jasper through.

Once inside, he closed the gate and unclipped the lead. For a moment, he rested his forehead against Jasper's. "You're going to like it here. You'll have all you can eat and room to run. And I'll be here to take care of you. We're going to be all right."

No rocket-propelled grenades would be aimed at them. No Taliban terrorist would take them captive and leave them to die. They were on American soil. The land of the free and the brave where people could live in peace.

Except when serial killers attacked women.

Parker wasn't quite sure what he'd signed up for. Travis had mentioned he was being hired for all the training he'd received in the army. Outriders were people who'd known combat, had unique and honed fighting skills, and wouldn't hesitate to defend, rescue or extract people who were victims of threats or violence.

But serial killers? Wow.

COWBOY JUSTICE AT WHISKEY GULCH

New York Times Bestselling Author

ELLE JAMES

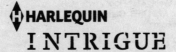

HARLEQUIN
INTRIGUE

For my father, who had the heart and morals of a hero and the
work ethic of a cowboy. He was the man who set the bar for all
other men in my life. He was a quiet guy who loved his family
and would do anything for us. I love and miss you, Dad.

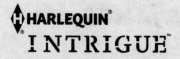

Recycling programs
for this product may
not exist in your area.

ISBN-13: 978-1-335-58216-4

Cowboy Justice at Whiskey Gulch

Copyright © 2022 by Mary Jernigan

For questions and comments about the quality of this book,
please contact us at CustomerService@Harlequin.com.

Harlequin Enterprises ULC
22 Adelaide St. West, 41st Floor
Toronto, Ontario M5H 4E3, Canada
www.Harlequin.com

Printed in U.S.A.

Elle James, a *New York Times* bestselling author, started writing when her sister challenged her to write a romance novel. She has managed a full-time job and raised three wonderful children, and she and her husband even tried ranching exotic birds (ostriches, emus and rheas). Ask her, and she'll tell you what it's like to go toe-to-toe with an angry 350-pound bird! Elle loves to hear from fans at ellejames@earthlink.net or ellejames.com.

Books by Elle James

Harlequin Intrigue

The Outriders Series

Homicide at Whiskey Gulch
Hideout at Whiskey Gulch
Held Hostage at Whiskey Gulch
Setup at Whiskey Gulch
Missing Witness at Whiskey Gulch
Cowboy Justice at Whiskey Gulch

Declan's Defenders

Marine Force Recon
Show of Force
Full Force
Driving Force
Tactical Force
Disruptive Force

Mission: Six

One Intrepid SEAL
Two Dauntless Hearts
Three Courageous Words
Four Relentless Days
Five Ways to Surrender
Six Minutes to Midnight

Visit the Author Profile page at Harlequin.com.

CAST OF CHARACTERS

Parker Shaw—Former Delta Force soldier captured and tortured by the Taliban and medically retired. He goes to work for Trace Travis and the Outriders.

Abby Gibson—Elementary school teacher who escapes her abductors and is compelled to go back and save others who weren't so fortunate.

Trace Travis—Former Delta Force soldier who shares his inheritance with his father's bastard son and builds a security agency employing former military personnel.

Irish Monahan—Former Delta Force soldier who left active duty to make a life out of the line of fire. Working for Trace Travis as a member of the Outriders.

Matt Hennessey—Prior service, marine and town bad boy, now half owner of the Whiskey Gulch Ranch and the Outriders Agency.

Sonny Tackett—Handsome young sheriff's deputy new to Whiskey Gulch.

Rachel Pratt—Missing young mother of two who was abducted when she got a flat tire.

Laura Owens—College student abducted at a truck stop on her way back to school.

Roy Felton—Former felon out on parole working odd jobs where he can.

Brandon Marshall—Real estate agent who knows the county and the people in it.

William Dutton—Local car dealer who drives expensive cars and wears fancy suits.

Prologue

Parker Shaw was greeted with silence as he swam up out of the darkness. He stared at the stars in a clear night sky and wondered where the hell he was.

When he tried to move, pain radiated throughout his body. He lay back panting, his head swimming, his vision fogged by a gray haze.

A breeze swept over him, carrying the scent of smoke and aviation fuel, sending a rush of images through his confused mind.

Afghanistan.

The mission…kill…who?

Lying as still as possible was the only way to keep the pain at bay.

Kill who?

Taliban leader Abdul Akhund.

Memories rushed in.

They'd gone into the town, made their kill and were on their way out to their extraction point when all hell broke loose.

The alarm went out and a dozen Taliban came out of the woodwork.

They'd barely made it to the field where the helicopter was to pick them up. Once all six Deltas were on board, the pilot lifted off the ground.

The rest was a little fuzzy.

There was a loud bang…the aircraft shuttered… and dropped from the sky.

Parker lifted his head enough to see the wreckage of the helicopter a few feet away. His heart raced and he struggled again to move. Pain ripped through his leg, ribs and arm. Hell, everything hurt. But he had to get to the helicopter.

With one hand, Parker pushed to a sitting position. His other arm hung at his side, useless. His head spun, the cuts on his arms burned and the throb in his leg was excruciating.

When he tried to stand, only one leg worked, the other too injured to support his weight. The only way he could get to the chopper was to drag himself.

He dug the fingers of his good hand into the dirt and pulled himself toward the mangled wreckage, the knot in his gut nothing to do with his injuries. He knew before he reached the mass of twisted metal what he'd find.

Amid the crushed fuselage lay his friends, his team, the men he considered brothers.

No sounds rose from the wreckage. No moans of the dying. Those trapped inside had died instantly upon impact. The only reason he'd survived was because he'd been thrown.

Shouts and an engine's rumble disturbed the silence.

Unable to walk, much less run, Parker turned away from the destruction and dragged himself away.

Headlights pierced the darkness. A truck rolled to a stop beside the helicopter. Men with AK-47s dropped out of the back and surrounded what remained of the chopper, with Parker having made it a mere twenty feet away.

With the Taliban surrounding the downed Black Hawk, it was only a matter of time before they discovered him.

He lay still, facedown, and played possum.

With his injuries, he'd just as soon be dead.

A shout sounded and footsteps pounded the earth, heading toward him.

He couldn't fight back. He didn't have a gun. His knife was still in the sheath around his waist, but he couldn't fight off at least half a dozen armed Taliban. If he wanted to survive, he had to remain "dead."

Peering through his eyelashes, he watched as each of the men gathered around him, all talking at once.

Parker's Pashto was sketchy at best. From what little he understood, they were wondering if he could be alive.

One man poked his side with the barrel of his rifle, hitting one of Parker's injured ribs.

With every ounce of control, Parker fought to keep from making a sound or from flinching.

As if still unsure, the guy nudged him with the toe of his boot. Then pushed harder until Parker was rolled onto his back.

In Pashto the man said, "These are the men who killed Akhund."

One of the Taliban terrorists dropped to his haunches and pulled at the buckles on Parker's body armor, then jerked it off his body.

Bolts of pain ripped through Parker, driving him to the edge of a blackout. He must have moaned.

The Taliban fighter jumped back, holding the bulletproof body armor to his chest and called out in Pashto, "He is alive!"

A taller guy gave the order. "Take him."

Too injured and broken to fight back, Parker continued to feign unconsciousness, hoping his deadweight would deter them from carrying him to wherever they had in mind. He needed to stay with the chopper. Eventually, a team would be sent out to recover the bodies.

If taken by the Taliban, they might never find his body. He had no doubt they'd end up killing him.

Two men hooked their hands beneath Parker's shoulders and hauled him to his feet.

The pain shooting through his arm and injured leg made him pass out, only to come to while being dragged toward the truck.

Parker was in big trouble. His team had taken out Akhund to rid Afghanistan of one of the most ruthless terrorists the Taliban boasted of. Akhund's MO had been to torture, drag his prisoner in front of a camera and then behead him.

Parker couldn't run. His leg was most likely broken. He couldn't fight, his shoulder seemed to be dislocated, and his ribs felt like someone was piercing him with a hot poker.

If they were going to behead him, he hoped it would be soon. It couldn't be any worse than the torture he was already facing.

The pain sent him in and out of consciousness.

He came to again when they dropped him in the dirt in front of the pickup's tailgate.

The largest, meanest looking man in the group grabbed his hair, yanked his head up and said in Pashto, "You are one of the infidels who killed Abdul Akhund."

Yeah, you moron, Parker thought. He closed his eyes and pretended to pass out.

The man holding his hair backhanded him across the cheekbone and released his grip on Parker's hair.

Parker crashed to the ground and lay there, hoping they'd think he was dead and leave him alone.

That wasn't to be.

A booted foot kicked Parker in the ribs. If they weren't already broken, they would be now.

Once wasn't enough. The man kicked him again.

After the fourth kick, Parker grabbed the man's foot with his good hand and pulled it out from under him.

The man came down hard on his backside.

The other men surrounded him, kicking wherever they could get a foot in.

Parker balled into the fetal position, covering his head the best he could with his one good arm, the other lying uselessly beneath him. Agony racked his body to the point he had to disassociate himself from what was happening.

His vision blurred as he teetered on the verge of blacking out, yet again.

The big guy shouted, and the kicking ceased.

Parker sucked in a labored breath, pain knifing through his chest with even the slightest movement.

He was grabbed again beneath the arms and hauled to an upright position, dangling between the men holding him.

The big guy punched him in the face several times and then in the gut.

Blood dripped from a cut above his eyebrow, blinding one of Parker's eyes. The other had been hit enough it had begun to swell, making it difficult to see.

If not for the sound of a helicopter, the men would have continued to hit him. Instead, the one who was apparently in charge shouted orders to the terrorists holding him.

They tossed him into the back of the truck, jumped

in with him and took off, headed away from the crashed chopper and the village where the Delta Force team had met their mission objectives.

Parker needed to stay at the crash site. It was the only way a rescue team would be able to find him. However, with two men holding on to him, Parker had no way of escaping.

Through the slit of his swollen eyelid, he watched as the dark silhouette of a Black Hawk helicopter appeared on the horizon, heading toward them.

The Taliban driver hit the accelerator, picking up speed, taking Parker farther away from his chance of rescue. His only hope disappeared in the cloud of dust the truck kicked up behind them.

If he survived whatever the terrorists had in store for him, he was on his own to get back to friendly forces.

The truck headed into the hills on a dirt road that curved through a narrow valley. Every rut, bump and swerve hit Parker with a fresh jolt of torment.

When the vehicle finally stopped, the leader appeared at the end of the truck bed, carrying a machete. He waved it at the men and ordered them to take their prisoner to the top of a hill.

This was it. The point at which he'd be beheaded.

They dragged him out of the vehicle. When his legs hit the ground, the jolt of pain made him black out. Not for long enough.

At the top of the hill, they dropped him in the dirt.

The big guy chopped limbs from a scrubby tree with a machete and created four stakes. He handed them to the men with instructions to pound them into the ground. Then they tore off Parker's uniform jacket, ripped it into long strips, and tied them to the stakes.

Parker fought the best he could with one arm and one leg. It took four men to hold him down, while two more tied his wrists and ankles to the stakes.

Their leader stood over him with the machete, his eyes narrowing, his lip curling into a feral sneer as he leaned over and slid the machete across Parker's side and then over his broken leg, leaving two lines of blood. "He will die a slow death as the birds feast on his flesh."

Then he spat on Parker, turned and left. His men followed. The sound of the truck engine echoed off the hills, slowly fading away.

Parker lay in the silence, the cool night air biting his exposed flesh. Blood seeped from the wounds in his side and thigh and he thanked the Lord for sparing him the beheading.

He wouldn't give up. No, sir. Not while there was fight still left in him.

For thirty minutes, maybe an hour, he lay still, gathering strength, working at the bindings around his wrist. He pulled and tugged, slowly trying to wiggle the stake loose in the ground, until the stake finally pulled free.

Fueled by that little bit of success, he pressed his

hand to the wound in his side. The blood had congealed. He could do little until he freed his other wrist and ankles. Beyond that, he didn't dare think. A man with a broken leg, left alone in the hills, had little chance of survival.

Parker rolled to his side, the broken ribs shooting a fresh kind of hell through his body. He reached for his other wrist and yanked at the bindings. The stake came free quicker than the last.

He lay back in the dirt, breathing raggedly. For a long moment, he considered how much easier it would have been had the Taliban cut off his head. But that would mean they'd won. When he survived and made it back to friendly forces, he would thumb his nose at the men who'd left him to die.

Pressing his good arm to his chest and side, he struggled to sit up, failing twice before succeeding. He bent his knees and scooted on his buttocks toward the stakes holding down his ankles. Then he leaned over and reached for the one holding his broken left leg.

Because his legs were spread wide and bending over hurt his ribs, he had a difficult time reaching with his right hand. Eventually, he snagged the binding and jerked hard, leaning back as he did.

Sweat popped out on his forehead. Through the stabbing pain in his ribs and leg, he persevered until the stake slid free of the hard-packed ground.

Not taking a break from the pain, he worked the

other leg free. With only one functional hand, he didn't bother to untie the bindings from around his wrists and ankles. However, he was able to slip the stakes free at the other end.

A broken leg and a dislocated arm would make it impossible for him to get far. The rescue team would have located the crashed helicopter. Hopefully, they would have extracted his fallen brothers and realized they were one short.

His throat tightened as images of his teammates' bodies, trapped in the wreckage of the Black Hawk, flooded his mind. He should have died with them. But he hadn't. Eyes burning, he vowed to live because his fallen comrades would have expected that of him. To honor their deaths by living the life he'd been spared.

Maybe walking out of the hills and all the way to the forward operating base wasn't reasonable. But if he could let them know where he was without alerting the Taliban, he might have a chance.

Over the next twenty-four hours, he put his plan in place, dragging his broken body over the rocky hilltop inch by inch, gathering, arranging and creating a message his country would see, but not the Taliban. If they were looking.

When he was done, he found a spot in the middle, lay down and covered his body in dirt to help combat the chill of the night air and slept.

Morning dawned, waking him with the bright

light of the sun rising on the eastern horizon. His leg throbbed and his ribs burned with every breath he took. What he wouldn't give for a drink of water. With the daylight, he started to second-guess his decision to send a message.

How long should he wait for help to arrive? Should he find a way to get himself out of the hills and back to the FOB? Or was it like getting lost in the forest? Should he stay in one place and let the search party have a better chance of finding him? When they didn't find his body in the wreckage, they'd either assume he'd escaped. Or they'd assume he'd been taken to an unknown location in a Taliban-held village.

He'd give his message another day and then try to get himself out of the hills.

With the pain of his injuries slowing his progress, he used his one semi-functional arm to drag himself around the top of the hill, searching for anything he could use to splint his broken leg.

The area was dotted with sparse vegetation consisting of a few short bushes and one gnarled tree— about four feet high with crooked branches—leaning toward the southeast side.

At the edge of the hill, Parker looked down into the valley below. A few taller trees reached for the sun. If he made it to the bottom, he'd have to climb back up to wave down any helicopter or airplane that might fly over.

If a friendly aircraft didn't fly over in another

day, he'd drag himself to the valley for straight sticks to use as splints and a crutch. In the meantime, the crooked limbs would have to do. They'd be hard enough to acquire as it was.

He spent the next hour pulling himself up the side of the gnarled tree and breaking off limbs. Then he worked the knots loose on the ties around his ankles and used those strips of cloth to wrap around the limbs he'd pulled from the tree.

His dislocated arm hung useless throughout.

When he had his leg sufficiently splinted, he pulled himself up to stand by the tree. Then he wedged the knotted end of the fabric around the wrist of his bad arm into a fork between low branches near his knees.

He gritted his teeth, held his breath and leaned back. Pain shot through his arm into his shoulder. By leaning back, he could pull the dislocated arm downward. It wasn't enough. Parker pushed up onto the ball of his good foot, raising his shoulder higher, the knot in the fork of the tree pulling his arm further down.

The joint slid back into the socket.

The searing pain was replaced by a dull ache. Parker eased off the tension and disengaged the knot from the fork. He raised the injured arm and flexed his elbow, finally able to use the arm and hand again.

His success lifted his spirits and hardened his determination to survive.

As the sun set on the day, he lay down in the hollow he'd dug in the middle of his message and covered his body with dirt, using both hands.

Hungry, thirsty, exhausted, his splinted leg aching, he lay for a long time staring up at the sky blanketed by stars. He told himself that the hunger and pain were a reminder that he was still alive.

When morning came, he'd start his crawl down to the valley, where he'd find a long stick to use as a crutch. Then he'd walk back to the FOB.

He felt as if he'd just closed his eyes when the distant thump of rotor blades echoed against the hillsides.

Parker's eyes popped open, and he sat up.

The dark silhouette of a helicopter appeared over the top of a hill headed his way.

His pulse quickened and he scrambled to brush the dirt away from his body. Then he staggered to his feet, the pain in his leg nearly bringing him back down. Fighting back dizziness, he managed to remain standing. If only he had a flashlight or flare. Were they headed to another mission, or were they looking for him?

The helicopter flew over the top of his hill and disappeared over the next one.

Parker's heart sank to the pit of his belly.

Okay, Plan B was to start the long trek back in the morning. Maybe he should start at night. The sooner he made it back, the better. He wouldn't last very long without food. Even less time without water.

He squared his shoulders, pressed his hand to his broken ribs and took a step toward the edge of the hill.

Pain shot up his leg as he placed even the smallest amount of weight on it and hopped back onto his good leg.

Poised to repeat the effort, he paused.

The Black Hawk reappeared, heading straight for his hilltop.

Parker stood still. His breath caught and held in his lungs as he watched.

The chopper didn't slow until it was within five hundred feet of his position. Then it hovered and sank slowly to the ground.

The gunner aimed his machine gun out the side door.

Parker raised his hands.

Several soldiers leaped to the ground, weapons ready, and established a quick perimeter. Two more jumped out and ran toward him.

Parker remained upright.

"Sergeant Shaw?" one of the men asked in a distinct Southern drawl.

"Yes, sir," Parker croaked.

The man grinned and draped one of Parker's arms over his shoulder. "Thank God. I'm Grove, the flight medic. That's Skeeter. We're gonna get you back to the FOB."

The other man slipped Parker's other arm over his shoulder.

He winced and bit down hard to keep from moaning.

Together, they carried Parker between them back to the helicopter.

"When we didn't find you in the crashed helicopter, we thought we never would," Grove said. "Then we got coordinates leading to your SOS and were told we might find our missing Delta here."

Skeeter chuckled. "Smart move, man."

"How you managed to make that big a sign was amazing. Given your injuries, even more so," Grove said.

They eased him down onto the floor of the helicopter. "Lie down. We're going to get you started on an IV," Grove said as the perimeter guards climbed aboard, and the helicopter lifted into the air.

"Wait." Parker held onto Grove's arm and leaned toward the open door of the helicopter for one last look at the hill where the Taliban had left him to die.

As the Black Hawk rose higher, he could see the message he'd written in the large rocks he'd found an abundance of on that hill.

Grove shook his head, grinning. "I don't know how you did it."

Parker wasn't sure, either. But it had worked.

Skeeter nodded. "That's the biggest damned SOS I've ever seen."

"And the first time I've seen an SOS actually save a life," Grove said as he eased Parker onto his back.

"Don't worry. We've got you now. You're going to be all right."

Parker had fought so hard to make it to that point, pushing through the pain. Surrounded by US soldiers, he finally gave in.

His last thought as he faded into unconsciousness was, *I lived for them.*

Chapter One

Six months later

Parker pulled his truck and horse trailer to a stop at the side of the ranch house and shifted into Park. Tired, sore from sitting for so long on the three-day trip from Virginia to Whiskey Gulch, Texas, he dreaded stepping out of the truck. When he'd stopped the day before, his leg had given him hell. Hopefully, it wouldn't this time.

Not in front of his old friend and new boss. He could show no weakness.

A nervous whine reminded him that Brutus needed to stretch as well. It had been several hours since their last rest stop. The sleek silver pit bull stood in the passenger seat, his entire body wagging since he didn't have a tail to do the job.

Parker opened the door and slid to the ground, careful to hold on to the door until he was sure his leg wasn't going to buckle.

It held and he opened the door wider.

"Brutus, come," he commanded.

The dog leaped across the console and stood in the driver's seat, his mouth open, tongue lolling, happy to be there. Happy to be anywhere Parker was.

Ever since Parker had rescued him from his previous owner, Brutus had been glued to his side, a constant companion and eager to please him in every way.

Parker wasn't sure who'd rescued whom. When he'd found Brutus tied to that tree outside a run-down mobile home, starving, without water and in the heat of the summer, he'd known he couldn't leave the animal. He'd stopped his truck, climbed down and limped toward the dog, hoping he wouldn't turn on him and rip him apart.

Brutus had hunkered low to the ground, his head down, his eyes wary. He had scars on his face and body, probably from being beaten. A couple of the scars were round, like someone had pressed a lit cigarette into his skin.

Parker had been sick to find the dog so abused. He'd unclipped the chain from Brutus's neck. Holding on to his collar, he'd limped with the dog back to the truck.

Brutus's owner had yelled from the door. "Hey! Thass my dog."

Parker had helped Brutus into the truck. The animal could barely make it up. He was too light for his breed and all skin and bones.

The owner had come down from the trailer and

stalked toward Parker, barefoot, wearing a grimy wifebeater and equally dirty, worn jeans.

Parker had shut the truck door and faced the man.

The guy reeked of alcohol as he stopped in front of Parker and pointed at the truck. "I said thass my dog."

"Not anymore." Parker leveled a hard look at the man. "He's coming with me."

"The hell he is." The drunk had lunged for the door.

Parker grabbed his arm, yanked it hard and twisted it up between the man's shoulder blades.

"What the—" the man had whimpered, standing on his toes to ease the pain. "You got no right to steal a man's dog."

"You had no right to abuse him. Now, I'm taking him, or I'm calling the sheriff to have you arrested for animal cruelty." He ratcheted the arm up a little higher. "Which is it to be?"

The drunk danced on his tiptoes. "All right. Take the damned dog. Can't afford to feed him anyway."

Parker shoved the man as he released his arm.

The drunk spat on the ground at Parker's feet. "Mutt has no fight in him. The only thing he was good for was a bait dog. He never earned the name Brutus."

Rage burned through Parker. He'd swung hard, catching the drunk in the gut.

The man bent over and fell to his knees.

Parker had fought the urge to pummel the man

into the dirt. He had to tell himself he wasn't worth going to jail over. And that would leave Brutus homeless.

"Touch another dog and I'll be back to finish the job," Parker warned.

The drunk had vomited and remained on his knees in the dirt as Parker climbed into the truck and drove away.

Brutus had lain on the passenger seat, staring at him all the way to the veterinarian's office, unsure of Parker, probably wondering if this human would beat him as well.

That had been three months ago, shortly after the removal of Parker's leg cast and his move to the Hearts and Heroes Rehabilitation Ranch.

The therapists at the ranch had been hesitant to bring Brutus on board. They'd eventually allowed him to move into Parker's cabin after he'd spent a three-week quarantine period with the veterinarian, taken all his vaccinations and worm meds, and was declared free of fleas.

Parker reached out and scratched Brutus behind the ears. In the three months since he'd rescued the pit bull, the dog had gained twenty pounds, learned to sit, stay, roll over and shake.

More than the tricks, Brutus had helped Parker through therapy. Their walks got longer and longer as both veteran and dog recovered their strength.

Parker stepped back from the truck and tapped his leg, the signal for Brutus to heel.

The dog jumped down from the driver's seat and sat at Parker's feet, looking up at him, eager to please.

"Parker Shaw," a voice called out from the porch of the ranch house.

Parker looked up as Trace Travis stepped down and closed the distance between them.

The former Delta Force operator held out his hand. "I'm so glad you finally arrived. I was beginning to worry you had truck or trailer troubles."

Parker gripped his hand. "Not at all. We made a couple of extra stops along the way to exercise our legs."

Trace pulled him into a quick hug. "It's been a long time."

"Yes, it has," Parker said. Memories of the last time he'd seen Trace surfaced. "We were a good team in Syria."

Trace nodded. "Yes, we were. I miss the guys. I didn't want to take the transfer."

"We missed you, too." Parker's heart constricted in his chest.

"I was sorry to hear about Patch, Griz and Mort." Trace stepped backward. "I'm glad you're still among the living."

Patch, Griz and Mort were three of the men who hadn't made it out of the crash that had damaged Parker's leg and earned him a medical discharge from the army.

Trace nodded toward the trailer. "I have to admit, I never knew you rode horses."

Parker snorted. "I didn't, until three months ago. The rehab ranch the VA sent me to also rehabilitates horses. I learned there."

"Horses have a way of getting into your blood, heart and soul." Trace grinned. "And I guess you liked it well enough to get one of your own."

Parker shook his head. "I didn't like it at first. Too painful." He tapped his bum leg. "Then I met Jasper. Half-starved, when he came to the ranch shortly after I arrived. He wouldn't let anyone touch him. My therapist challenged me to work with him." Parker reached down to scratch Brutus's ears. "Like the dog, Jasper just needed someone to give a damn. He still won't let anyone else touch him. But he lets me."

"It takes an incredible amount of time and patience to gain a horse's trust," Trace said.

Parker snorted. "I had plenty of time. I learned the patience." The pounding of a horse's hoof against the floor of the trailer made Parker turn toward the trailer. "Speak of the devil. I need to let him out and get him some food and water. He's had it rough the past few days, cooped up in that trailer."

Trace tipped his head to the side. "Bring him to the barn. He can have a stall while you feed him and there's a pasture you can let him run in afterward."

Parker backed Jasper out of the trailer and walked with him, Brutus and Trace to the barn.

Trace chuckled. "I've never hired anyone who accepted my offer on the condition I accept his horse and dog as part of the bargain."

"We appreciated it," Parker said. "These two beasts have been through a lot. I wouldn't have deserted them."

Trace opened the barn door and held it for Parker as he led the dun gelding inside. "Your devotion to your animals made me want you here even more. When you're not working a case, you'll be working the ranch." He followed them in and hurried to open a stall door. "We all do."

"Good." Parker said. He led Jasper into the stall and unclipped his lead, grabbed the water bucket from a hook on the wall and left the stall, closing the door behind him. "I like to keep busy. It helps keep my mind off...things."

"I get that." Trace nodded toward a spicket over a large sink against the wall. "Water's over there. You give Jasper sweet feed and hay?"

Parker nodded. "Half a bucket of feed, two sections of hay." He filled the water bucket and returned to the stall, hanging the bucket on a hook in the wall.

Jasper went to it immediately.

Parker rubbed the side of the gelding's neck and scratched behind his ears. "You're going to like your new home."

"Sweet feed first." Trace handed the bucket of feed over the stall door.

Parker poured the bucket of feed into a small trough nailed to the wall.

The gelding nudged him aside in his impatience to get to his dinner.

Parker laughed. "Greedy, are we?"

"Here's the hay." Trace handed the two sections of hay over to him.

Parker stuffed the sections of hay into the corner hay rack and stood for a few minutes, watching Jasper finish the sweet feed and move on to the hay. Parker enjoyed the earthy scent of horses and hay. "Have you already got an assignment for me?"

Trace leaned over the stall door. "Not yet. I wasn't exactly sure when you'd be ready to work. I figured you'd need a couple of days to get settled in and meet the others."

"I'm ready as soon as you have work for me. I don't need time to settle." He didn't need time to ruminate on his losses. The dead weren't coming back. However, the nightmares did. The less he thought about the past, the fewer bad dreams.

"I have plenty of ranch work to do, if staying busy is your goal. In fact, tomorrow morning, I was going to have Irish ride the fences to the south to make sure they're still intact. We've had feral hogs plowing through some of them. They tear them up and then they come in, destroy the land and kill the smaller livestock like goats and calves."

"I could get started riding the fences today," Parker said.

Trace shook his head. "It's already late afternoon. Jasper needs to run free after being on the road for so long. And my mother and Lily have dinner on the table. I want you to meet some of the members of the Outriders. Most of them are from my former Delta Force team."

"Are there any Deltas left in the army?" Parker gave Trace a crooked grin. "Are you hiring all of them?"

"I promise," Trace held up a hand. "I didn't take all of them, though I'm sure I could keep quite a few busy."

"That much business?" Parker asked.

"Yes. We can come back out after dinner to let Jasper out in the pasture." Trace led the way back to the house.

Parker followed him to the back porch and hesitated on the bottom step. "I'm not real good company lately. I've spoken more to Brutus and Jasper than people." His therapist had called him out on that during his last session.

"You don't have to stay at the table. If you want, after a quick introduction, you can excuse yourself. I can have Lily prepare a plate for you if you prefer to eat alone."

"That won't be necessary." Parker didn't like being treated differently. His issues dealing with others had more to do with the grief he still felt for the loss of his brothers. And guilt for not having died with them in the crash.

His physical injuries had healed over the past six months, but Parker had a way to go with the mental and emotional ones.

Other than getting stiff from the long drive, he

was almost back to his normal self. Although he wouldn't say he was happy, he was no longer sad or angry all the time.

Brutus and Jasper helped him focus on something else besides his last mission with Delta Force. Sometimes even the animals didn't relieve him of the grief. Both the dog and the horse could sense when depression threatened to take him to a dark place.

Trace waited at the door without saying a word, allowing Parker to make up his own mind.

Squaring his shoulders, Parker climbed the steps and passed through the back door into the kitchen.

Voices sounded from deeper in the house. Someone laughed and others joined in.

A surge of longing built inside Parker. He hadn't laughed since the crash. He hadn't realized how much he missed it until now. Wanting to see the source, he followed Trace through the kitchen and into a formal dining room with a long narrow table down the center.

At the far end sat a woman with salt-and-pepper hair and blue eyes. She stood and waved him into the room. "You must be Parker," she said, coming around the others at the table to take his hand. "So nice to meet you."

"Parker Shaw," Trace said, "This is Rosalyn Trace. My mother."

"Parker, has Trace shown you around the house yet?" she asked.

Parker shook his head. "I just walked through the door."

"That's fine. After dinner, I'd love to show you around and take you up to your room where you can unpack and get comfortable."

"Thank you, ma'am," he said.

She smiled up at him. "You don't have to call me ma'am. You may call me Rosalyn." She turned to a petite blonde with big blue eyes. "Parker, this lovely lady is my soon-to-be-daughter-in-law, the only woman who could possibly handle my son." She smiled at the blonde. "Lily."

Parker shook hands with Trace's woman. "Pleasure to meet you."

She grinned up at him. "I hear you brought your own horse." She glanced down at his feet. "And dog."

Parker glance down at Brutus. "I'm sorry. I didn't realize he'd come in with me. He sticks to me like a fly to honey. I'll take him back outside."

Mrs. Trace waved toward Parker. "It's okay. As long as he's housebroken, he can stay."

"He is," Parker assured her.

Trace went around the room, introducing the others. "I'm not sure if you've met Joseph Monahan. He's former Delta Force."

The man grinned. "Call me Irish."

"I don't recall meeting you, but it's nice to meet you now." Parker and Irish met halfway and exchanged a greeting and a handshake.

Irish turned to the woman beside him. "This is Tessa, my fiancée."

Parker dipped his head. "Nice to meet you, ma'am."

Trace waved to a man with black hair and brown eyes. "Levi Warren, another member of my team and former Delta, meet Parker Shaw."

The two men exchanged a handshake.

"My woman isn't here because she's sleeping. She has the graveyard shift tonight with the sheriff's department," Levi said. "You'll meet her soon enough. Look for Deputy Dallas Jones."

"I will," Parker promised.

Trace pointed to a man with sandy-blond hair who raised a hand from the other side of the table. "Becker Jackson, former Delta, and his better half, Olivia Swann."

"She's definitely my better half." Becker smiled down at the dark-haired woman beside him and turned to raise a hand. "Welcome aboard, Shaw."

Finally, Trace turned to the man at his side who resembled Trace with his dark brown hair and green eyes. "And this is my brother, Matt Hennessey."

Matt held out his hand. "Glad you've joined us." He slid his arm around the redhead beside him. "And this is Aubrey, my girl."

Aubrey smiled and shook Parker's hand.

"Now that the introductions have been made, please, have a seat." Rosalyn waved toward an empty chair.

Trace held Lily's chair as she settled back in.

"We weren't sure when you'd make it, so we started without you," she said and passed a platter of grilled steaks his way.

"I'm glad you did." Parker selected a steak, the scent making his stomach rumble. "I wasn't sure when I'd make it, either. The wind was playing havoc with the trailer. I had to take it slow."

"Right decision," Lily said. "And the three of you made it intact as a result."

"Lily is a great help. She and my mother have managed the ranch by themselves."

His mother's mouth twisted. "Barely. Thankfully, you're home now and we have more help." She frowned and waved a hand at Trace. "Make sure Parker gets a potato and some of those green beans."

Trace stabbed a fork in a baked potato and dropped it onto Parker's plate. Then he passed the bowl of green beans. "The point is, if you have any questions about the ranch, they can answer it better than I can."

Lily stood, grabbed a pitcher of iced tea and came around to fill Parker's glass. "That's not entirely true." She went around the table filling the glasses of others at the table before taking her seat again. "Trace has stepped right back into ranch life since he left active duty."

"Maybe so," Trace said. "However, I spend a lot more time managing my team of Outriders, which leaves much of the ranch management to you two."

Lily exchanged a nod of acknowledgement with her mother-in-law. "True. But it's nice to have help."

Trace cut into the steak on his plate and pointed his fork at Irish. "Irish, about riding the southern fence tomorrow—"

"Yeah, about that," Irish said. "It'll have to wait until I get back from the ranch supply store. We need more field fence and barbed wire."

Trace leaned his head toward Parker. "I think it would be a good opportunity for Parker to get out and stretch his horse's legs. He can ride the southern fence line and identify where we need to mend and what we'll need."

"Rosalyn and I are going with Irish to the supply store and stopping for groceries on the way back," Lily said. "Otherwise, I'd show Parker around."

"And I have a truck engine to reassemble for a customer," Matt said.

Parker frowned. "Truck engine?"

Matt gave him a crooked grin. "Before I became a part of the Trace family, I owned an auto repair shop. I still dabble in it when I'm not on an Outrider mission."

Rosalyn smiled. "Matt isn't just a mechanic."

"He's prior military," Trace said.

Parker cocked an eyebrow. "Branch?"

"Marine," Matt said.

"Marine Force Recon," Irish corrected. "He's just as spec ops as the rest of us Deltas."

Levi lifted a hand. "I can ride with Parker part

of the way, but I'll have to come back early. I meet with my new client tomorrow afternoon."

"Good," Trace said. "I have a meeting with the sheriff in the morning. I can postpone it, but I'd rather not."

"Is the ranch completely fenced?" Parker didn't like feeling like someone had to babysit him. "If so, I would rather find my way around by myself. No one needs to walk me through."

"There are several gates to go through," Rosalyn said. "I can draw a rough sketch of them."

"That's all I need. If I get turned around, I can use the GPS on my cell phone to find my way back."

"If you get hurt, don't count on placing a phone call," Trace said. "Cell reception is spotty, the further you get away from the house."

"Noted," Parker said. He spent the rest of the meal eating quietly and listening to the conversations around him.

Tessa was a nurse at the local hospital. Aubrey was a home health care nurse. The two women spoke of some of the challenges they faced and how they handled them.

Matt and Trace discussed the feral hogs and the damage they'd done to a neighbor's fences and his boar goat herd.

"I saw one of the hogs last night on my drive back from town," Matt said. "It was as big as a cow."

"And meaner," Trace said. "You don't want to

run across one on foot. They're fast and they're car-
nivores."

"And they're not picky about what kind of flesh
they eat." Lily caught Trace's attention. "You remember Fred Sarley."

"Who's Fred Sarley?" asked Parker. He hadn't
meant to intrude on the conversation, but he couldn't
deny his curiosity. Besides, he needed to know what
he was up against.

Trace frowned. "A farmer on the south side of
town. Had a lot of pigs."

"Had?" asked Parker.

Lily nodded.

"Do I even want to know?" asked Parker.

Lily exchanged a glance with Rosalyn. "No. He
disappeared. The sheriff and half the town searched
for him, but all they found was a single dingo boot
next to his hog pen." She shook her head. "When
they gave up looking, they turned to the hogs in the
pen. They examined the contents of the boars' bel-
lies and found bits of clothing and human flesh. They
ran the DNA and found Fred." Lily looked around
the table and grimaced. "Sorry. Not the best topic
at the dinner table."

"Old man Hersh said the hogs have put a big dent
in his herd of boar goats. He's lost at least ten kids
and four does. He's setting out traps to catch them
before they do more damage."

Finishing his meal before the others, Parker laid
his fork and knife on his plate and looked around.

"If you'll excuse me, I'd like to check on my horse and let him out into the pasture."

"I'm done here," Irish said. "I'll go with you. I want to check on one of the horses."

"Just leave your plates in the sink," Trace said. "It's my night to pull kitchen patrol duty."

Parker and Irish carried their plates to the sink, rinsed them and set them to the side.

Together, they walked out the back door, Brutus at their heels.

"I'm surprised we didn't run into each other on active duty," Irish said. "I haven't been out for long."

Parker shot a glance toward the other man. "I remember your call sign being mentioned, but I never forget a face. We haven't actually met before today."

"Trace says you were medically discharged."

Parker's lips pressed together. He tapped his left leg. "Helicopter crash did a number on my leg. The army has no use for a Delta who can't pass an army physical fitness test."

"You're getting around pretty well. I don't even notice a limp."

"Physical therapy, riding Jasper, and walking Brutus helped."

"Got family?" Irish asked.

Parker shook his head.

"Mom died of breast cancer when I was in high school. Dad had a heart attack two years ago."

"No wife…kids?" Irish chuckled. "Tell me to shut up if I'm being too nosy."

"Shut up." Parker grinned. "Seriously, I never married. Never had time, with the army. As far as I know, no kids. I have two younger sisters, though." He glanced toward Irish. "What about you? Were you forced out, too?"

Irish shook his head. "No way. I got out on my own terms before I took too many hits, or some terrorist tagged me." He looked out across the pasture. "I wanted to start living the rest of my life."

"And is working with Trace and the Outriders helping you get there?" Parker asked.

Irish's face split into a huge grin. "Absolutely. I wouldn't have met Tessa had I not come to Whiskey Gulch. I never knew I could love someone as much as I love her. She was actually my first assignment as an Outrider."

Parker's eyebrows dipped. "No kidding?"

"Yeah." His grin faded. "She was the target of a serial killer. She managed to escape him but didn't see his face. It was my job to protect her and help find out who the killer was."

"I take it you caught him?"

Irish nodded, his jaw tightening. "He almost killed Tessa. He's not going to hurt another woman, ever again."

"Your first assignment was a success." Parker shook his head. "Are all the assignments that intense?"

Irish's shoulders relaxed. "No. But there have been some close calls. For a small town, Whiskey Gulch has had its share of drama. Now, Becker recently took a job that started here in Whiskey Gulch. He went undercover in Dallas with Olivia to take down an art thief and kidnapper."

"I guess our training will come in handy after all."

"Exactly." Irish opened the barn door and held it for Parker.

Irish crossed the barn to the stall where Jasper pawed the ground with his hoof, eager to get outside to run. He snapped the lead onto the animal's halter and opened the gate.

Jasper pushed through and headed for the open barn door.

Parker pulled him up short. "Which pasture should I release Jasper in?"

"If you'll hold up a minute, I'll show you." Irish opened a stall door across from the one Jasper had been in and stood beside a bay horse. He bent, lifted the right front hoof and studied it carefully. He let go, straightened and snapped a lead on the horse's halter. "Sweetheart, you get to run."

He joined Parker in the middle of the barn, leading the mare. "She stepped on a nail a week ago. It had gotten infected. She needed time for it to heal where I could check on it daily. Poor girl's been in the barn since." He patted the mare's neck. "Thankfully, it appears to have healed nicely."

He led the mare out. "I'll let her loose with the other ranch horses. You can put your horse in the empty pasture until he acclimates and familiarizes with the others across the fence."

Parker opened the gate Irish indicated and led Jasper through. Once inside, he closed the gate and unclipped the lead. For a moment, he rested his forehead against Jasper's. "You're going to like it here. You'll have all you can eat and room to run. And I'll be here to take care of you. We're going to be all right."

No rocket-propelled grenades would be aimed at them. No Taliban terrorist would take them captive and leave them to die. They were on American soil. The land of the free and the home of the brave, where people could live in peace.

Except when serial killers attacked women.

Parker wasn't quite sure what he'd signed up for. Trace had mentioned he was being hired because of all the training he'd received in the army. Outriders were men with unique combat skills who wouldn't hesitate to defend, rescue or extract people from threats or violence.

But serial killers? Wow.

He rubbed his hand along Jasper's neck and then stepped back.

The horse nudged him once, turned and trotted out into the middle of the field, tossing his head. Free from the trailer and loving his new home.

Parker slipped through the gate and secured the latch.

Irish joined him and lifted his chin toward the

horse galloping along the fence. "He's going to like it here." He turned to Parker. "You will, too. What better place to use our skills? And we have put those skills to use and will again. We never know who we'll be up against. We're in south Texas. We could run into drug cartels, mafia, human traffickers, serial killers, you name it."

"How soon do you think I'll get my first assignment?" Parker asked as they walked back to the house.

"Soon, I'm sure." Irish laughed. "Sometimes the jobs fall into our laps. In Matt's case, his ran out in front of him on the highway. He almost ran her over. Don't worry. You'll get yours soon enough."

Parker hoped so. He'd been away from the action long enough.

Irish glanced at the clouds building in the western sky. "Looks like we might get some rain. We sure can use some. But don't hold your breath. The weather around here is a big tease. Big clouds, dump in the next county and leave us dry here." Irish climbed the stairs.

Parker looked to the west in time to catch the flash of lightning on the edge of a thunderhead growing in size and intensity.

It would be a rough night for Brutus. The poor guy shook uncontrollably when there was a thunderstorm.

Thunder rumbled in the distance.

Brutus whined and leaned his stout body into Parker's legs.

Parker reached down and patted the dog's head. "Come on, old man. Let's get some rest. Tomorrow's the beginning of our new life here in Texas."

Chapter Two

"Abby?" A shaky voice called out in the darkness. "You awake?"

Abby lay curled in the wire cage on the threadbare, dirty blanket, shivering in the drafty air of the attic. "I am," she whispered. "You hanging in there, Rachel?"

The young mother sniffled. "Barely."

"Thinking about Tommy and Allissa?" Abby asked.

"Yes. I can't stop thinking about them." The woman's voice broke on a sob. "I shouldn't have stopped to change the flat tire. I should have driven it all the way to a town. And my babies... My poor, sweet babies..." Rachel sobbed, the sound weak after days of being held captive in a cage, in the drafty old house that smelled of dust and mildew.

"Rachel, you can't beat yourself up," Abby insisted. "You didn't ask for this. The people who did this own the blame."

"God, I hope someone found my babies and got

them home to my husband. They must have been terrified. And Tommy… I hope he stayed in the car. He's so little and yet so mature for a four-year-old. If he wandered out onto the road…"

"He's okay, Rachel," Abby tried to assure her. "You have to believe that and focus on staying alive and well for when we're rescued."

"Rescued?" Cara Jo snorted from the cage on the other side of Rachel's. "Like that's gonna happen. No one knows we're here. No one is even looking for me. No one cares." The seventeen-year-old had been a runaway living on the streets of San Antonio when she'd been snatched.

"Cara Jo," Rachel said, "your family loves you. They have to be wild with worry."

"No. I was just a stupid kid to them. And I proved them right. I ran away with Marty, my boyfriend. Too dumb to know how good I had it at home."

"What happened to Marty?" Abby asked.

Cara Jo laughed without humor. "He got smart and went home."

"Why didn't you?" Rachel asked.

"Remember the part about me being a stupid kid?" Cara Jo sighed. "I was too stubborn. I didn't want to admit I was wrong and they were right."

"And now?" Abby asked.

"I'd give anything to see my parents again." The teen spoke so softly Abby almost didn't hear her words. "I had come to that conclusion and had just reached the highway to hitch a ride home when I was taken."

"We're going to be rescued, aren't we?" Laura, the college coed, asked. "Someone has to find us. Surely they'll find my car and look for me."

"If someone didn't steal it and drive it down to Mexico to be sold there," Cara Jo said. "Were your keys still in it when you stopped for gas?"

"Yes," Laura said. "Along with my purse, laptop and all of my schoolbooks. I had midterms coming up. I shouldn't have gone home for the weekend. I'd still be in San Angelo. Not...here."

"*Mi madre* must be heartbroken," Valentina whispered. "We love each other so much. She will have searched the road between the bus stop and *mi casa*, looking for me. I knew better than to talk to a stranger." She paused. "He was so handsome and looked like a nice man. I believed him when he said he was lost and needed help with directions."

"I got caught with the same tactic," Cara Jo said. "Was the guy who snatched you blond with blue-gray eyes?"

"Yes," Valentina said. "He was."

"The guy who stopped to help me wore a ball cap," Rachel said. "I didn't notice what color his eyes or hair was. I was more worried about getting my tire changed and my kids home before dark. We still had another couple of hours to go before we reached New Braunfels. I was pulling stuff out of my trunk when he slipped a bag over my head and threw me in the trunk of his car."

"I was pumping gas at a truck stop," Laura said. "A white van pulled up close to my car. I was putting the pump handle back when someone grabbed me from behind and threw me in the van. They put a bag over my head. I never saw their faces."

"What about you, Abby," Rachel asked. "Did you see who grabbed you?"

"No," she said. "We'd taken two classes of fifth graders to visit the cowboy museum in Kerrville. We'd stopped at a rest area on the way back to eat our sack lunches and use the restrooms. I was waiting outside the boys' restroom for two of our children. The others had all loaded onto the bus. I was approached from behind. He slipped a cloth over my mouth. I tried to fight him, but whatever was on the cloth knocked me out. I woke up in this cage. Never saw who took me. And, like Rachel, I haven't stopped worrying about the children that were still in the bathroom."

"Why are they keeping us?" Valentina asked in the darkness.

"Haven't you heard of human trafficking?" Cara Jo said. "They're either going to sell us or pimp us out. The question isn't what they're going to do to us. It's when."

A flash of muted light made it through the sheet hung over the only window in the attic. Seconds later, thunder rumbled in the distance.

Abby had spent the days staring at the window, imagining herself breaking free of the cage, throwing open the window and sliding down the roof to the ground below.

If she could just get to that window, she'd find a way out of the attic.

The only time the women were released from their cages was to relieve themselves once a day. Their jailer would be up soon to take them, one at a time, down to the only bathroom in the house. A bathroom with no windows. They'd been stripped of their warm clothes and shoes, only allowed to keep the shirts and underwear they'd been wearing when they were taken. Abby wore the bright blue school T-shirt each of the teachers and children had worn for the field trip. Her shirt hung down just below her hips.

Abby had thought they'd be found within the first couple of days. After the third day came and went with no law enforcement officers breaking down the doors, she realized help wasn't coming. She'd only been there for three days. Some of the others had been there longer.

Three days? A week? She couldn't wait to be saved. She had to do something to save herself.

Her wrists were zip-tied in front of her, the plastic straps digging into her skin, chafing it raw. She'd scraped the plastic along the metal the cage was made of, hoping to weaken the plastic. If she could get her hands free, she might find a way to work the lock loose on the front of her cage.

If she made it out of the house, she'd be running barefoot in a T-shirt. Hopefully, she wouldn't have to go far to find a house and someone with a telephone she could use to call 911.

More light flashed through the sheet. Abby could see the other women, each trapped in the kind of cage in which people kenneled their dogs. Each of the cages had padlocks on the front to keep the doors secure.

With the storm moving closer, the lightning flashed more frequently, thunder following.

Footsteps sounded on the wooden staircase leading up to the attic.

Abby braced herself. So far, the men who'd captured them hadn't hurt them. But how long would that last? If Cara Jo was right, they were collecting women for human trafficking or the sex trade.

A shiver rippled through her. The nights were the worst. Fall had come to Texas and with it, cooler temperatures. The T-shirt did little to keep her warm. She pulled her legs up to her chest, tucked her knees under the shirt and waited for the door to open.

A key scraped in the lock on the door and the old handle squeaked as it turned.

The man in the ski mask appeared in the doorway, carrying a flashlight. He shined the light into each of the cages.

The women blinked as the beam blinded them.

He crossed to the cage closest to him.

Abby's.

As he squatted in front of the gate to remove the padlock, Abby pulled her legs in tighter, getting ready.

As soon as he lifted the lock off the hasp and swung the latch to the side, Abby slammed her feet into the gate.

The wire door hit the jailer in the head, the motion tipping him over. He lost his balance and fell backward.

Abby lunged through the opening, scrambled to her feet and raced for the door.

"Run, Abby!" Cara Jo yelled.

Through the door and down the stairs, Abby flew, gaining momentum she'd need to get her out of the house and away.

At the bottom of the stairs, she passed the door to the bathroom and kept going. Even before she reached the front door, she skidded to a stop. The door had boards nailed over it on the inside.

Abby spun and raced toward the back of the house, passing through what must have been the living room. The only light shining on the first floor came from a portable, battery-powered lantern sitting on a flimsy table next to a folding lounge chair, like the ones her grandmother used to have in her backyard. Pizza boxes and beer cans littered the floor.

Footsteps pounded down the stairs.

Her heart in her throat, Abby ran through an ancient kitchen to the back door. Grabbing the handle in her bound hands, she yanked it open and ran into a wall of muscles and flesh.

Thick arms clamped around her and lifted her off her feet.

She kicked and screamed, fighting her hardest. Lightning flashed and thunder drowned her screams as the man carried her back into the house and set her on her feet. He wore a black ski mask like the man who'd dealt with them for the past few days.

The captor rushed forward and grabbed her from behind. He wrapped one arm around her middle and clamped a hand over her mouth.

"We only offer the best and healthiest. Look for yourself." The man who'd stopped her at the door spoke in a deep, gravelly voice. He stepped aside and another man moved closer, this one wearing a white Halloween mask like that of a serial killer from a horror film. He wasn't as tall as the other two, but he was big and barrel-chested. A fringe of salt-and-pepper gray hair peeked out around the mask.

Abby tried to wriggle free of the arm around her.

The man lifted her off the ground, dangling her in the air.

When the man in the white mask came closer, Abby kicked out, catching him in the face.

He staggered backward and fell on his backside, his hand scraping against the doorframe.

The man who'd been talking about her reached down and pulled the white-masked man to his feet.

"Sorry. She's a wild one. But don't worry, we'll provide sedative for transport."

White-mask guy stood stiffly, brushing his hands over his tailored suit and rubbing a scratch on the back of one of his hands. "She'll do," he said. "We promised five. What else have you got?" His voice boomed through the old house.

Doorstop guy jerked his head toward the stairs. "Take her up and bring down another."

The jailer spun her around, flung her over his shoulder and carried her back up the stairs. He dumped her on the floor and reached for a long metal rod that had been hung on the wall.

"In the cage," he commanded.

When Abby refused, he touched the wand to her skin, sending a jolt of electricity burning through her body. She jerked and leaped back.

He stepped toward her and held up the rod. "In the cage."

Still tingling, the pain fresh on her mind and skin, Abby backed another step, then turned and crawled back into the cage. Angry tears slipped down her cheeks as he fit the lock in place, sealing her inside.

Lightning flashed as he unlocked Laura's cage and motioned for her to proceed down the stairs ahead of him.

"Are you okay?" Rachel whispered.

"Yeah." Abby rubbed the sore spot on her arm.

"What happened?" Cara Jo asked.

"I ran out the back door and was stopped by a second guy who was followed by another." She pressed her lips together. "You're right, Cara Jo. They have a potential buyer downstairs."

Cara Jo cursed, Rachel gasped and Valentina sobbed.

"I'm not giving up," Abby vowed.

The man took each of the women down to the buyer one at a time and brought them back to the attic. Valentina was last, crying all the way.

By the time they'd all been paraded in front of the three men, the storm was on them in full force.

Thunder boomed so loudly it shook the rafters. Abby fully expected the lightning to rip through the roof of the old house at any moment. She'd use the clash of the thunder to her advantage.

As soon as the idea entered her head, another took its place. Abby bunched her legs close to her chest and waited for the next bolt of lightning.

Light flashed.

Abby kicked the front of her cage as hard as she could.

"What are you doing?" Rachel demanded.

"Getting out of here." Abby tugged the ragged blanket out from under her and wrapped it around her feet. She pulled back her legs and waited.

Lightning flashed.

She kicked.

As the storm raged, Abby kicked.

Just when her feet had reached their limit and

she was about to give up, she forced herself to kick one last time.

Lightning struck close by, followed immediately by a long rumble of thunder that rattled the timbers of the old house.

As the thunder boomed, Abby kicked.

The front of the enclosure crashed to the floor.

She scrambled out of the cage. Using a technique she'd seen on the internet, she slammed her wrists down, pulling her hands apart at the same time, and snapped the zip tie free.

Then she ran to Laura's cage.

"You can't unlock them," Cara Jo said. "You have to get out and bring back help."

"I can't leave you." A heavy weight settled on Abby's chest as she pulled at the padlock on Laura's cage, knowing Cara Jo was right.

The college student touched her fingers through the wire. "Go. Get help."

Abby pushed to her feet. In the flashes of lightning, she ran toward the attic window and yanked off the sheet. She struggled to lift the window. It moved a little but not enough. Abby ran back to her broken cage, grabbed the blanket, wrapped it around her arm and rushed back to the window.

In the next flash of lightning and boom of thunder, she slammed her arm through the glass and wiped the shards clear of the windowsill.

When she leaned out, her stomach roiled.

The constant flashes of lightning revealed a steep

roof that only took her part way to the ground. She'd have to free-fall the last ten feet.

"Hurry," Rachel urged. "He's coming."

Footsteps sounded on the stairs as thunder crashed around them.

Abby tried again to raise the window. She managed to get it up a couple of inches. She quickly fed the blanket through the gap between the window frame and the windowsill and then brought the empty window frame down on the blanket. Hopefully, it would hold the blanket long enough for Abby to climb down the steep roof.

"Go, Abby," Cara Jo whispered.

"Go," Laura entreated.

Abby climbed through the broken window, lowered herself slowly, grabbed the blanket and slid downward, using the blanket like a rope. Rain poured down, soaking her, blowing into her face and dripping from her hair into her eyes.

She ran out of fabric a few feet short of the roof's edge.

In another flash of lightning, she looked up and blinked the rain from her eyes. Her heart stalled in her chest.

The captor leaned through the window and grabbed for the blanket.

Abby released her hold on the blanket and slipped the last couple of feet down the roof and over the edge, falling ten feet to the ground.

When she landed, her feet sank into mud, her legs

buckling beneath her. Abby fell backward, landing hard, the air knocked from her lungs.

Rain pounded her face and body, the cold seeping through her skin to her bones.

For a long, precious second, she lay there, trying to force air back to her lungs.

She gasped, rolled over, pushed to her feet and took off. A quick glance over her shoulder showed her what she already knew. The man was no longer hanging out the window. He'd be running down the stairs and bursting through the back door any minute.

With only the lightning to illuminate her way, she ran, ignoring the pain in her bare feet. Every rock and stick took a toll. All she could hope was for the soles of her feet to go numb. She couldn't stop until she had enough distance between her and the men who'd kidnapped her and the other women.

Her lungs burned as she ran. No matter which direction she looked, she couldn't find any lights. The old house must have been isolated.

Abby climbed hills and slid down into valleys. She trudged on, hoping to find any sign of life. As exhaustion took hold, she started to fear she was walking in circles and would wind up back where she'd started.

She stumbled through a broken fence and staggered several more feet before she dropped to her knees too exhausted to take another step.

The rain had moved on. The clouds were breaking up, allowing some stars to shine through.

Abby looked around. She couldn't stop now. She had to hide, or risk being found. When the sun came up, she'd move on and find a house, make that call and send people to rescue the others.

Abby moaned as she stood, putting pressure back on her ravaged feet. Every step was excruciating. She made it as far as a slight crevice in the ground where a tree had been blown over, roots and all. She lay in the hollow where the roots had once been and scraped leaves and dirt over her, covering her body and face. As she positioned the last leaves over her face and then her hands, her world faded to black.

Chapter Three

Having napped cramped in his truck two nights straight, Parker found it almost heaven to sleep stretched out on a comfortable bed that fit the entire length of his big frame.

After reassuring Brutus through a nasty thunderstorm, he'd slept so soundly that the rattle of Brutus snoring on a rug beside the bed hadn't disturbed him. He woke as the gray light of predawn chased away the darkness in the room he'd been assigned in Trace's home.

With a sense of purpose, he eased his legs over the side of the bed and sat up. Even his leg felt better after elevating it for seven hours.

Parker pushed to his feet, stretched his arms toward the ceiling and performed his morning physical therapy exercises to keep his muscles flexible. With Brutus at his side, he'd gotten to the point he could walk five miles easily and he could ride for hours on Jasper. Running was taking a little longer.

He could go for up to two miles before the pain became unbearable.

His doctor had told him his running days were over. Parker refused to accept the diagnosis. In the back of his mind, he harbored a—perhaps delusional—belief that if he could pass the army physical fitness test, they'd let him back in.

Logic told him it wasn't possible. Not only had he sustained a leg injury, but the traumatic brain injury from the crash also continued to plague him. No. He wouldn't be invited back into the Delta Forces or the army.

While at the rehab ranch, he'd applied for a number of jobs all over the country…he and a hundred other candidates. Not one interview had come of it. Who needed a man whose only skill sets were centered around combat? Because of his injuries, he couldn't even go into city or state law enforcement.

Parker pulled on his jeans, walked to the French doors, pushed them open and stepped out onto an upper deck that wrapped around the back of the house. From where he stood, the view spread before him, past the barn and out across a pasture. The hills beyond were shrouded in fog.

Jasper grazed contentedly, keeping close to the gate Parker had led him through the day before. The overnight thunderstorm had delivered much-needed rain, leaving residual moisture in the air. Thus, the low-level fog that would burn off after sunrise.

Refreshed and ready to start his new job, Parker

shaved, brushed his teeth and combed his hair. After dressing in a faded denim shirt, jeans and his army boots, he slung a leather shoulder holster carrying his 9 mm pistol over his arms and buckled it across his chest. He might need to borrow a rifle scabbard he could attach to his saddle in case he ran across the feral hogs Trace and Lily had discussed at the dinner table the night before.

When he was ready, he grabbed a light jacket and descended the stairs with Brutus at his side. Parker made it his first mission of the day to find coffee. He could go without breakfast, but coffee was a necessity.

The fragrant aroma of fresh-brewed java led him to the kitchen where Rosalyn leaned against the counter, sipping from a mug, her eyes closed.

He paused at the entrance, not wanting to intrude on her quiet time.

She opened her eyes and smile. "Good morning, Parker."

He dipped his head. "Morning, ma'am."

"Fresh coffee. Nothing like it. If you want some, you can help yourself. The mugs are in the cabinet above the coffee maker. For that matter, whenever you're hungry, you can help yourself to anything in the kitchen. Make yourself at home."

"Thank you." Parker strode across the floor, found a mug and poured a full cup. His first sip warmed his insides all the way down to his empty belly. Best way to start a new day, a new job and a new life. He could handle anything as long as he started the day with a cup of joe.

"I'm about to cook breakfast for everyone." Rosalyn said. "You will join us, won't you?"

"No, ma'am. I'm good with just coffee."

"Might be a long day. A good breakfast can take you all the way to dinner."

He nodded. "Yes, ma'am. I know."

Her lips twisted in a wry grin. "Look at me, trying to mother the new guy when he's a grown man." She set her mug on the counter. "Ignore me. Old habits die hard."

He liked Mrs. Travis. She seemed nice and obviously cared about others. "Thank you. I'll take you up on breakfast another day. I want to check on my horse and get an early start to the day. Might take me a while to find my way around."

Rosalyn straightened. "That reminds me, I made a layout of the land, the fences and gates. You won't miss the gates. There are tire ruts leading up to all of them. But you'll need to know which ones lead off the ranch, so you don't get lost on someone else's property."

She crossed to a far counter, retrieved a sheet of paper and returned to where Parker stood, sipping the hot coffee. Laying it on the counter, she oriented the drawing to the north. "You'll want to go through these gates to get to the southern border fence. Irish thinks the hogs are getting across in a low-lying area around here."

She drew her finger along the line about two thirds of the way to the back of the property. "I'm sure you won't have difficulty finding the breach or navigating your way back to the ranch house." She left the paper on the counter and reached into a lower cabinet for a large, cast-iron skillet. "I'll have scrambled eggs ready in fifteen minutes if you change your mind. You can saddle your horse and come back for sustenance."

"Thank you, but I'll head out as soon my horse is ready."

"We might still be in town when you get back, though we're aiming to be home by noon. I have a ham in the fridge for sandwiches. The bread is in the pantry and condiments in the fridge."

"Thank you," he said and finished the last drop of coffee. Parker carried the mug to the sink, rinsed it and placed it in the dishwasher. "I'll see you later, ma'am."

She smiled. "Please, call me Rosalyn. *Ma'am* sounds so formal and we're anything but formal around here."

"Yes, ma'am—Rosalyn." He settled his cowboy hat on his head and headed for the back door. As soon as he pulled open the door, Brutus was out and running across the yard toward the barn. He didn't stop until he stood at the fence surrounding the pasture where Jasper had spent the night.

The horse trotted over and lowered his head, sniffing at the dog.

Brutus's entire body wagged as he greeted the horse. The two had become friends at the rehab ranch, establishing a special bond.

Parker bypassed the horse and dog and headed into the barn.

Someone was already there, cleaning a stall. He couldn't see who.

Curious, he headed over to see if whoever it was needed help.

He found Lily, wearing scuffed dingo boots, jeans and a T-shirt. She scooped up soiled straw with a hay fork and tossed it into the wheelbarrow close to where Parker stood. Her eyes rounded when she spotted him. "Sorry. I didn't know you were standing there."

"You need help?"

Lily shook her head. "This was the last stall. If you want to push the wheelbarrow out to the compost pile behind the barn, I'd appreciate it. I've already fed the animals and filled the water troughs." She exited the stall, hung the hay fork on the wall and dusted straw from her jeans. "I was just about to head for the house, a shower and breakfast. Will you be joining us?"

He shook his head. "I had coffee with Ms.—Rosalyn. I want to get a start finding my way around."

Lily nodded. "Don't get lost." She left the barn.

Parker grabbed the handles of the wheelbarrow and pushed it through the barn door and around to the back where he dumped the contents onto a pile of soiled straw. After rinsing the barrel using a hose outside the barn, he leaned it up against the barn to dry.

Jasper whinnied.

Parker glanced across at the horse with the dog sitting patiently at its feet. He ducked into the barn, scooped feed into a bucket and poured it into the trough in the stall. Then he grabbed a lead rope off a hook and returned to Jasper.

"How about a bite of sweet feed before we get started?" He clipped the lead on the horse's halter and led him into the barn.

Brutus kept pace, careful not to get under the horse's hooves.

Parker released Jasper into the stall he'd occupied the previous afternoon and closed the gate. While the horse consumed the feed, Parker went out to his trailer for his bridle, saddle and blanket and carried them into the barn.

By then Jasper had finished his snack.

Parker snapped the lead on his halter, led him out of the stall and tied him to a post.

He found a brush in the tack room and went to work grooming the horse. Jasper stood patiently, swishing his tail occasionally.

When he was finished brushing Jasper, Parker tossed the saddle blanket over the animal's back, followed by the saddle. He cinched the girth and let the stirrup fall into place.

Jasper shifted from hoof to hoof in anticipation of going for a ride.

Parker unhooked the lead, slipped the bridle over the animal's nose, fitting the bit between his teeth, then slid the straps over Jasper's ears and fastened the buckles.

Brutus turned circles beside Jasper, eager to get out and run.

Parker would make sure he stopped often enough to let him rest. On a couple of occasions, he'd hoisted the pit bull up into the saddle with him. The dog would be fine. Parker would make sure of that.

He led Jasper out into the barnyard and over to the gate Rosalyn had indicated he should go through on his way to the southern edge of the property. Once through the gate, he mounted Jasper and nudged the horse into a trot.

The fog hung low over the field, making it difficult for him to see the gate at the other end. Old tracks in the ground indicated vehicles had probably been driven through the field on the same path over the years. Figuring it was probably the path leading to the next gate, Parker followed it.

Brutus ran alongside, darting off every once in a while to chase a moth or a bird.

Eventually, the path led to a gate.

Parker took the opportunity to dismount and stretch his sore leg as he opened the gate and led Jasper through.

Back in the saddle, he followed the path, wondering if he should have waited at the ranch house until the fog lifted. He'd wanted to explore the ranch. Unfortunately, he wasn't seeing much of it as it was blanketed in misty fog.

Based on Rosalyn's directions, he had one more gate to pass through and an open expanse of fields and hills before he reached the southern end of the ranch. When he reached it, he leaned over without dismounting and unlatched the gate. He rode through and leaned down to close the gate. It was a new task for Jasper. He danced sideways several times and then settled, allowing Parker to close and latch the gate without dismounting.

Parker had been riding for almost an hour when Brutus bolted and raced ahead.

"Brutus!" Parker yelled. "Heel!"

The dog either ignored Parker's command or didn't hear it. He disappeared into the fog.

Parker, worried Brutus would get lost on the vast ranch, urged Jasper to pick up the pace.

Ahead, Brutus's silvery form materialized out of the fog. He stood beside a fallen tree, his body tense, the hackles raised on the back of his neck.

Parker squinted into the fog, trying to catch a glimpse of whatever had Brutus riled.

Brutus held his position even as Parker rode Jasper up to where the dog stood.

The pit bull snarled, staring into the fog, his growl more menacing than anything Parker had heard since he'd adopted him.

Shadowy figures moved in the fog. They were big, hulking creatures.

Parker tensed and slipped his hands beneath his jacket, his fingers curling around the handle of his Glock. He pulled it free and held it out.

A herd of feral hogs emerged from the fog, headed toward Parker, Brutus and Jasper.

FIERCE GROWLING INTERRUPTED her nightmare of waking up in an animal cage, cold, hungry and scared. Or was she still asleep and the animal wanted his crate back?

Abby cracked an eye open and looked up through a veil of leaves. Where was she? Why was she covered in leaves?

The growling persisted. Too loud to be her stomach. A shiver shook her body, dislodging some of the leaves over her face, and she stared up at the razor-sharp teeth of a snarling dog.

Her heart slammed against her ribs and adrenaline shot through her veins. Fear gripped her, robbing the air from her lungs. Every instinct told her to run.

Logic followed, urging her to think before she acted. If she lay perfectly still, maybe the rabid dog would go away and leave her to live another day.

Another shiver consumed her as the damp earth beneath her and the cool morning air sank into her bones.

Though the dog stood over her, it looked in another direction, not toward her. It took a step forward, snarling viciously.

When it moved, another animal's face hovered over her. This one didn't snarl, but it was huge and could crush her if it chose.

Its nostrils twitched as it leaned closer and sniffed her face with a velvety nose.

A horse.

The beast ducked its head lower. Abby stared past the horse's head to the man seated in the saddle holding a gun.

They'd found her. The evil monsters from her nightmare had found her.

She couldn't let them take her again. The others were counting on her to get help. She had to get help to free them.

The dog growled low and wicked. A moment later it darted away, barking as viciously as it growled.

Abby rolled out of the shallow hollow up onto her hands and knees and then launched herself away from the dog, the horse and the armed man.

She stumbled, righted herself and kept running toward a low bank of fog. If she put enough distance between her and the man on the horse, she might lose herself in the hazy mist.

Again, she stumbled, went down on a knee and started back up when something hit her in the middle of her back, knocking her to the ground.

Over her shoulder she heard the menacing rumble of the dog's growl.

Abby froze, afraid to move lest the dog rip into her with those razor-sharp teeth.

He continued to snarl and then broke into a fearsome combination of barking and growling, his paws firmly planted in the middle of her back.

The clip-clop of a horse's hooves moved closer.

Bang! Bang! Bang!

The three shots rang out so close the sound reverberated in Abby's head. She held her breath, waiting for the pain that would surely follow.

It didn't.

The dog on her back leaped off and raced into the fog barking furiously.

Cold, scared and exhausted, Abby pushed to her feet and spun to face the man on the horse.

He swooped in, grabbed her arm and pulled her up and across the saddle in front of him. Then he spun the horse around and shouted, "Brutus, come!" He nudged the horse and it shot forward.

Abby hung on as the horse raced across a field, up a hill and down into a valley.

She lay across muscular thighs, her head bouncing against a rock-solid calf.

When the horse finally slowed, Abby pushed against the man's leg and fought to be free.

He held onto her with a hand pressed against the middle of her back. "Stay still, woman."

Abby continued to kick and twist until the man lifted her, flipped her around. He sat her in his lap and clamped his arms around her, trapping her arms against her sides. "Are you just *trying* to get yourself killed?" he demanded, a frown creasing his brow.

"Let me go! I won't go back," she vowed.

"Damn right you're not going back. That herd of hogs would have had you for dinner. Why the hell are you out here, alone and half naked anyway?"

She stopped struggling and stared into the man's face. "You're not taking me back?"

"No. Besides the hogs, you're not dressed for wandering around the ranch. Where are your shoes and clothes?"

"You don't know?" She shook her head. "You're not one of them?" Her head spun and the little bit of control she'd held on to slipped. Tears welled in her eyes. "I'm safe?" she whispered.

The man frowned. "Of course, you're safe. But if Brutus hadn't found you first..." His frown deepened. "Those hogs would have."

She shuddered. The shudder turned to shivers and ended in her entire body trembling so uncontrollably that her teeth rattled in her head.

"Oh, hell," the man muttered and set her away from his chest. "Hold on to the saddle horn," he commanded.

Her hands shook as she wrapped them around the saddle horn.

The man shrugged out of his jacket and wrapped it around her body. Then pressed her against his chest, holding her in the circle of one arm. With his other hand, he gripped the reins and nudged the horse into a swift walk.

The jacket, warm from his body heat, helped, but not enough to stop the shakes. Her captivity, the escape, and lying cold in an earthen hollow through the night had taken their toll.

A gray haze closed in around her. The man, horse and fog blended together in the haze, and Abby gave in to the power of the darkness.

Chapter Four

When the woman went limp in his arms, Parker tightened his hold to keep her from sliding out of his lap onto the ground.

Her entire body was covered in mud. He couldn't begin to assess her injuries until some, or all, of the dirt was washed away.

Her skin was cold. At the very least, she was probably suffering from hypothermia.

His arm tightened around her even more in an effort to warm her cold body. He had to get her to the ranch house and into warm blankets or a warm bath to bring her body temperature up to normal.

He couldn't make the horse go any faster. The jolting motion of trotting or galloping might exacerbate the extent of her injuries. The ride back was excruciatingly slow. Several times, he wondered if it wouldn't be better to stop, build a fire and warm her there. What if she succumbed to hypothermia before they reached the Travises' residence?

Building a fire would only be a short-term solution. And there was the chance the hogs would find them. He needed to get her somewhere safe and warm where she could also be clean and dry. He could call for an ambulance from the ranch house. Based on the scrapes, cuts and bruises he could see, and how cool her skin was, she might need medical attention.

Juggling the woman in his arms, he struggled with the gates, managing to open and close them without dropping her in the process.

By the time he reached the ranch, his arm ached as much as his bad leg.

He tried to wake her long enough to get down from the horse, but she was completely out. It worried him. He slipped backward on Jasper, off the saddle and onto the horse's rump. Then he laid her across the saddle on her belly.

Once he was sure she wouldn't fall, he slid down Jasper's rump to the ground.

His bad leg buckled, pain shooting into his hip. Holding onto the horse's tail, he managed to remain upright until the feeling returned to his leg and he could walk almost normally.

He rounded to the side of the horse as the woman lying over the saddle moved. The movement caused her to slip. She fell backward into his arms. He scooped her up and carried her across the barnyard and up to the back porch.

Brutus followed, maintaining his vigil to protect Parker and the woman from the feral hogs.

Parker managed the door handle and pushed the door open with his foot.

"Hello," he called out.

No one answered.

He carried her into the huge living room and laid her out on one of the leather couches.

As he slipped his arms from beneath the woman, her eyelids fluttered open, and she stared up into his gaze. "Where…am I?"

"You're at the Whiskey Gulch Ranch. I'm going to call for an ambulance."

She shook her head. "No."

"Yes," he insisted. "You're not well. You could be suffering from hypothermia, dehydration or any number of things I'm not qualified to treat. I'm calling for an ambulance." When he started to straighten, her hand grabbed his arm in a surprisingly strong grip.

"You can't," she said, her hand still gripping his arm, refusing to let go. She closed her eyes and lay still. "I need to be dead," she whispered.

"What?" He eased down beside her and sat on the floor. "I don't understand. Why do you need to die?"

"So they won't know I'm looking for them," she shivered in his jacket, her body starting to tremble again. "Cold," she murmured.

"At the very least, let's get you cleaned up and warmed up. Then you can explain to me what you're talking about."

"Warm sounds good," she said. "Never b-been so c-cold."

He stood, lifted her in his arms and carried her up the stairs. Though his bad leg protested, he made it to the top and into his bedroom. He didn't stop until he was in the bathroom. "Can you sit up on your own?" he asked.

She frowned. "I think so."

He sat her on the toilet lid and waited to see if she would pass out.

When she didn't, he turned to the tub, plugged the drain and turned on the faucet. After adjusting the water temperature, he faced her and lowered himself to sit on the edge of the tub. "Are you hanging in there?"

She'd wrapped her arms around her middle, still shivering. "I'm alive. That's what matters."

His lips twisted. "First you wanted to be dead. Now you say alive is what matters."

"If they think I'm alive, they might kill the others. I can't let that happen."

Parker tensed. "Others?"

The woman nodded. "Four others. Two teenage girls and two young women." Her body shook so hard she nearly fell off the toilet seat.

Parker steadied her, then checked the water in the tub. "Look, we need to get you warmed up. You can tell me the rest when you're feeling better." He was thinking the sheriff might be interested in her story and he wanted to have it straight before he got the law involved.

"Can you get undressed and into the tub on your own?"

She raised her hands to pull at the jacket. They shook so badly she couldn't get it off.

"Here," he said. "Let me." Parker removed the jacket.

Her eyes widened when he reached for her again.

"Don't worry. You can keep the rest. I'm just going to help you into the water."

He scooped her into his arms and eased her into the warm water. "Too hot?"

She shook her head and smiled. "It's perfect." Her shivering slowed and finally stopped.

He turned to the cabinet, found a washcloth and sat again on the edge of the tub. He couldn't leave her for fear she'd pass out again and drown.

Parker dipped the cloth into the water and squirted bodywash onto it. "Mind if I clean off the dirt from your feet? Since you won't go to the hospital, we need to treat your cuts to keep them from getting infected."

"I should be able to do it myself." The woman bent her knees and tried to sit up. The effort appeared to be too much. She lay back in defeat, sending water sloshing over the edge of the tub.

He cocked an eyebrow. "I'd get one of the ladies of the house to do it, but they've all gone to town for supplies, and I have no idea when they'll return.

You could wait for them, but the water might get cold. Or we can go with the assumption a little dirt never hurt anyone."

She rolled her head from side to side. "No. I can't risk infection. I have to be well enough to find them."

"Is that a *yes, I'll accept a little help*? Or *no, I have no idea who you are, why should I trust you*?"

Brutus entered the bathroom and laid his chin on the rim of the tub, staring at the woman in the water.

She laughed, the sound catching on a sob. "I thought this guy was going to eat me alive." She reached out a tentative hand. "Does he bite?"

Parker's lips pressed into a tight line. "His previous owner thought he was useless as a fighting dog. He said he didn't have any fight in him." He laid a hand on the animal's back. "He was wrong. Brutus just needed a reason to fight. When he found you in the dirt, he held off a herd of wild hogs to protect you."

She frowned. "The three shots?"

Parker nodded. "To scare them off. They weren't as impressed with gunfire as they were with Brutus."

She extended her hand and let the dog sniff her fingers. "Brutus, huh? At least I know your name."

Parker shook his head. "I guess we've been a little busy getting you to this point. He held out his empty hand. "Parker Shaw."

Her brow furrowed as she placed her hand in his. "Abby Gibson." As quickly as she shook his hand, she drew hers back into the warm water and wrapped her arms around herself.

He held up the washcloth with the soap. "I'll understand if you're not comfortable with me washing your feet."

"It's just…" Abby looked away. "They were going to sell us." She pressed her fists to her lips and curled into a ball. "We were kept in cages the size of dog kennels." Her eyes filled with tears and her body shook with the force of retching sobs.

His jaw clenched and his chest tightened. Bastards. What made men so morally corrupt?

Her sobs continued.

Parker could take a beating or a bullet, but tears? He reached into the tub and pulled Abby out and onto his lap. Water went everywhere.

He didn't care.

This woman had been through trauma no human should have to endure. If he could, he'd take it all away. But the damage was done. All he could do was hold her and help her weather the storm of her memories.

The sobs slowly subsided. Her body cooled where it wasn't pressed to his and soon, she was shivering again.

He leaned her way from him and bushed a thumb over the tears on her cheeks. "You're okay now. I won't let them hurt you." Whoever they were. "Right now, you need to be warm." He helped her back into the tub.

She handed him the washcloth and looked up at him through red-rimmed eyes. "I'm sorry I've been such a burden." More tears welled and slipped down her cheeks. "But if you would… I would appreciate your help."

He took the cloth from her.

She leaned back in the warm water and closed her eyes, more tears slipping down her cheeks.

Parker reached into the tub and lifted one foot out and carefully washed her foot. With the dirt gone, the cuts and bruises were obvious. Some were already red and angry-looking. He worked the cloth up to her knees, identifying more abrasions that would need antibiotic ointment. Some needed bandages.

He stopped at the knee and laid her leg back in the warm water and lifted the next one.

The bottoms of her feet were ravaged from running barefoot through the Texas hill country. Sharp rocks, cactus and sticks had torn or bruised the uncalloused skin.

When he'd cleaned up to that knee, he rinsed the cloth, applied fresh bodywash and reached for the arm closest to him. As gently as before, he washed away the dirt and mud.

Her arms, like her legs, were covered in scrapes and cuts. When he put that arm back in the water, she offered the other.

He smiled and cleaned that one as well. By then, the water had cooled a little. It wouldn't be long before it got too cold. He rinsed the cloth again and pressed it into her palm. "Can you manage the rest?"

She nodded and struggled to sit up straight.

He stood. "Do you want me to leave you alone so you can finish?"

Her brow furrowed and a look of panic crossed her face. "No. If you don't mind, I'd rather you stayed." Her gaze went to the pit bull lapping up water from the floor. "And Brutus."

The dog looked up at the sound of his name.

"Okay. We'll stay."

Abby pressed the damp cloth to her face and washed away the dirt, grime and tears. Then she leaned back and sank all the way into the water until only her face remained above. She reached up and worked her fingers through her hair, stopping to let her arms rest.

Parker squirted shampoo into his hands and leaned over the tub. He worked the shampoo into her hair and massaged her scalp.

"I swear I'm not always this useless," she said, staring up at him with her face surrounded by shampoo bubbles.

"From what you've been through, I'll give you a pass." He winked. "Now tip your head back and let me work the suds out."

She leaned her head back in the water. Her long hair fanned out in the water as he rinsed her hair.

"There," he said. "You're on your own for the rest."

She reached out a hand and he helped her into a sitting position.

Abby stared down at the damp T-shirt clinging to her body. "I don't have any clothes to wear. They took them."

Another surge of anger ripped through Parker. When she was up to it, he'd get the full story from her. Then he'd go after the men who'd done this to her.

"I have some things you can wear." He reached into the cabinet with the bath towels, extracted a large, fluffy white one and laid it on the closed toilet seat.

He backed toward the door. "I'll get the clothes." Pausing at the door, he studied her face. "You sure you'll be all right on your own?"

She bit on her bottom lip for a moment and then gave him a weak smile. "I'll manage."

"Let me know when you want my help. I'll just be a few steps away." He looked down at Brutus. "Stay."

The dog sat on his haunches and stared up at him, waiting for his next command. "Good boy," Parker said and turned and walked toward the bathroom door.

"Parker?" Abby called out softly.

He looked over his shoulder.

"Could you leave the door open a little?" she asked.

"You bet." He stepped out of the bathroom and closed the door halfway. For a long moment, he stood there worrying that he'd come back in to find her passed out in the water.

The sound of her moving in the water reassured him that she was still conscious. And Brutus would alert him if she was in trouble. He left the door and crossed to the duffel bag he'd brought with him. That and a backpack contained all his worldly possessions. Everything else from his apartment outside of Fort Bragg had been donated to a homeless shelter. His move to Whiskey Gulch had been a chance to start over. To reinvent himself, to leave behind the only life he'd known since graduating high school.

Parker selected a clean black T-shirt and running shorts, figuring they might be the only things that might fit Abby. The shirt would hang down to her knees and the shorts would swamp her, but it was the best he could do.

"Uh… Parker?" Abby called out from the other room.

He hurried into the bathroom.

"I should be embarrassed," she murmured. "But I've never cared less about modesty than I do at this moment. Help." Abby still sat in the tub, only the T-shirt she'd been wearing was halfway over her head and stuck to her arms. Beneath it all was a matching bra and bikini panties in a soft shade of purple.

Parker gulped, his groin tightening automatically.

"I tried," she said from inside the fabric wrapped around her arms and head. "I. Just. Can't."

He dropped the shirt and shorts on the counter,

gripped the hem of the T-shirt and dragged it up her arms and off.

Immediately, she dropped her arms to cover herself, her cheeks flaming red. "Thanks."

He shook his head. "It's too late to be embarrassed. Let me help."

She nodded and reached out.

With his assistance, she stood and stepped out onto the bathmat. He wrapped her in the towel and helped to dry her off.

Once again, he scooped her up in his arms, towel and all, and carried her into the bedroom, settling her on the bed.

"Stay," he said to Brutus, who had followed them into the bedroom.

The dog sat beside the bed and waited for Parker to return from the bathroom, carrying the shirt and shorts.

Parker also brought another towel. He used it to pat the moisture out of Abby's hair. Then he fit the T-shirt over her head.

"Wait." Abby stopped him from pulling the shirt down over her body. "Turn around."

He frowned.

"I want to remove this wet bra," she said.

"Right." He performed an about-face.

A moment later, she said, "Okay. I'm decent."

When he faced her, she wore the T-shirt and held out the bra. "If you could hang this in the bathroom, I'd appreciate it."

Again, his groin tightened as he took the bra into the bathroom and hung it on a hook.

When he returned to the bedroom, she'd shimmied out of her panties and into the shorts. She was in the process of sliding between the sheets of the bed when he walked back into the room.

"Is it me or is it cold in here?" she said, her teeth clattering together.

"It's you." He helped her adjust the sheets and comforter around her, tucking it around her shoulders. Then he lifted her head, laid the driest towel on the pillow lowered her head and wrapped the towel like a turban around her damp hair. He laid the brush on the nightstand. "We'll tackle tangles later."

When she was covered from her toes to her chin, she looked up at him. "Thank you, Parker Shaw." She glanced down at the floor where Brutus sat patiently. "And thank you, Brutus."

Brutus took her mention of his name as an invitation for him to join her on the bed. He jumped up and settled beside her on the comforter.

Abby laughed and rested her hand on the dog.

"I'd be annoyed with him being on the bed, but I know how warm he can be," Parker said.

"He is warm." Abby blinked up at Parker, her eyelids drooping. "I need to find the others," she said.

"You need to rest," he said and sat on the edge of the bed. "When you're up to it, you can tell me everything. I'll help you find them."

Abby reached for his hand. "Promise?"

He nodded and gently squeezed her fingers. "I promise."

She brought his hand up to her cheek and closed her eyes. "Why should I trust you?" she whispered.

He chuckled. "I don't know. Why should you?"

Her lips curled in a smile. "You and Brutus saved my life."

"That was all Brutus," he said, liking the way her fingers curled around his.

She opened her eyes long enough to connect with his gaze. "Brutus didn't carry me back."

He smiled. "No, he didn't."

"You don't have to help me—" she looked up into his eyes "—but thank you."

"They say when a person saves another person's life, he's responsible for that person forever."

"Lucky me," she said with a crooked smile. Her smile faded. "For your sake, I hope it's not forever."

Parker stared down at the woman in his bed. He wasn't sure if she had fallen asleep or passed out again. Either way, she needed warmth and rest.

In the meantime, she was safe from whoever had kept her captive. He'd make sure she stayed that way.

Chapter Five

Abby lay scrunched in a fetal position, trapped in a cage while a storm raged around her. Footsteps pounded up the staircase leading to the attic where she and the other women were held hostage.

She had to get out of the cage and run before the kidnappers made it to the top. Abby pounded her feet against the cage door. Thunder boomed. The footsteps came louder as they neared the top of the stairs. With only seconds to spare, she kicked again, and the cage door broke free.

Abby scrambled out of the enclosure and pushed to her feet.

The door burst open, slamming against the wall.

One of the kidnappers in his black ski mask advanced toward her.

"No," she said inching away from the man. Her back bumped against the wall. Out of the corner of her eye she saw the window beside her.

Abby cocked her arm and knocked her elbow through the glass.

The man lunged for her, hitting her in the belly. Abby staggered backward and fell through the breached window, landing with a hard thump on her back, knocking the air from her lungs.

She blinked her eyes open to sunlight.

Hands slipped beneath her back and legs. "Hey, are you okay?" a deep, familiar voice spoke softly against her ear as she was lifted off the cool hardwood floor and deposited on the warm, soft comforter. Her body shook. Not from the cold, but from the panic of being confronted by one of the men who'd held her captive, by the nightmare of being held in a cage in the dark, the hope of rescue fading with each passing day.

Abby looked up into the eyes of the man who'd saved her. When he started to straighten, she gripped his arm.

He paused. "I take it you had a bad dream."

She nodded. "I was back in that attic. He was coming for me. I—I had to get away. Then I fell through the window and landed…"

"On the floor." Parker sighed. "Scoot."

She frowned.

He waved a hand indicating she should move over on the bed.

Abby eased across the mattress and slipped her legs between the sheets.

Parker kicked off his shoes, sat on the edge of the bed and swung his legs up onto the comforter. "Better?"

She stared up at him, frowning and unsure of this man or his intentions. "A little."

He opened his arms. "Come here."

Abby sat up and moved into his arms. As he wrapped them around her, she rested her cheek against his chest.

"Think you can tell me everything now?" he asked, his voice rumbling through his chest into her ear.

She nodded and started talking. As she explained about the field trip and abduction at the rest area, her fingers curled into his shirt.

His arms tightened around her reassuringly, giving her the courage to go on.

By the time she got through the part where she had escaped, her pulse pounded, and her gut knotted. "Then I ran until I could run no more."

"You're lucky you didn't break something in your fall from the roof," Parker said, stroking her drying hair. "And you're wrong."

"Wrong?" She tilted her head back and frowned up at him. "Why?"

"Brutus and I didn't save you." He touched a finger beneath her chin. "You saved yourself."

"I wouldn't be alive right now if you and Brutus hadn't shown up when you did." She laid her cheek back on his chest. "Now help me save the others."

"We're going to need help," he said.

Her heart beat faster. "No one can know I'm still alive. They'll move the others, hurry their sell or kill them." She looked up at him. "I couldn't get them out fast enough and had to leave them behind with the promise that I'd bring help." She shook her head. "I can't break that promise. None of them deserve what's happening to them."

Parker nodded. "I understand. But we're going to need help. You and I alone can't find them fast enough." When she started to protest again, he held up a hand. "Hear me out, will ya?"

She bit down hard on her bottom lip and nodded.

"I'm an Outrider. We're former military who help people, without all the rules and regulations that come along with government-run law enforcement." He smiled. "People like you and the women you want to save."

Her brow puckered. "What do you mean? Like vigilantes?"

He shook his head. "Security specialists. All with military training."

She laid her hand across his heart. "Do you trust them to keep my existence silent?"

He nodded. "These men are former Special Forces. We've had top-secret clearances and performed missions we can't talk about. Ever." He grinned. "I think we can keep a secret."

Abby drew in a ragged breath. "Okay. We could use all the help we can get."

The sound of doors opening and closing in the house below alerted Abby to the fact they no longer were alone in the house. "What will you tell them?"

"Exactly what you told me. They'll need as much information as possible."

Abby laid her cheek against his chest again, a shiver rippling through her body. "We have to hurry. I don't know how much time we have. Some of them had already been there a week. I was the last to arrive four days ago. Now that I've escaped, they'll probably move quick to keep from getting caught."

"Look, if you're okay on your own for a few minutes, I'd like to pull my boss aside and bring him up to speed on what happened." He tipped her chin up. "Will you be okay?"

She nodded.

"You'll be here when I get back?"

She frowned. "I'll be here. I have nowhere else to go."

"I just don't want you to go off and try to do this on your own."

She caught his arm. "No law enforcement?"

He shook his head. "No sheriff departments, police or FBI. We'll keep this operation on the down low."

"Thank you," she said. "I don't know what I'd have done if Brutus hadn't found me."

"I imagine you'd have found a way." He winked. "Rest and get your strength back. I'll be back shortly."

Parker left the room.

As soon as the door closed, the walls seemed to close in around her. Abby's breath caught and her pulse ratcheted up with the beginning of a panic attack. She pulled her hands out from beneath the comforter, knowing they were free of restraints, but she had to see them for herself.

She got out of the bed, her legs wobbling, sore and tired from her midnight run. For a long moment, she stood, letting her muscles adapt and legs steady before she crossed to the French doors. She reached for the handles, her heart racing, fully expecting the doors to be locked from the outside. When the handles turned, she let go of the breath she'd been holding and opened the doors, letting more sunlight stream into the room. She stood for a long time as the rays warmed her skin.

A cool breeze touched the bare skin of her legs, making her shiver.

Leaving the doors open, Abby returned to the bed and crawled beneath the comforter, her gaze on the open door and freedom.

Abby never wanted to be trapped in a cage, in the dark again. She'd rather die than live through that again.

She lay staring out at the sunshine, her arm hanging over the side of the bed to rest on Brutus's smooth back. Her last conscious thought before dreamless sleep claimed her was of the cowboy who'd swept her off her feet and carried her away from danger. The man was what heroes were made of.

PARKER DESCENDED THE stairs and went in search of whoever had returned from town, hoping it was

Trace. He desperately needed to talk to the man. Time was ticking by on the fate of four women.

He found Rosalyn in the kitchen unloading bags of groceries.

When he walked into the kitchen, she smiled. "Oh, Parker, back from riding the fence line already?"

He nodded. "Do you know when Trace will be back?"

"We ran into him in town. He said he'd be right behind us. He wanted to stop by Matt's shop for a minute about something the sheriff had told him. I expect he'll be coming through the door any moment."

"Thank you, ma'am."

She shook her head, her lips pinching. "Rosalyn."

"Rosalyn," he corrected. "Could you point me to the cabinet with the cups?"

She tipped her head toward one she passed as she carried a carton of milk to the refrigerator. "I was just about to make ham and cheese sandwiches for lunch. Would you care for one?"

"Yes, please," he said. "Could I get two?"

She laughed. "Absolutely. A man can work up an appetite riding fences."

He didn't want to tell her the other sandwich was for an unexpected guest. Not until he briefed Trace on the woman in his bedroom.

The sound of a truck's engine caught his attention.

"That's probably Trace now," Rosalyn said. "I'll

start on those sandwiches as soon as I finish putting away all the groceries. Irish and Lily are unloading feed and fencing supplies in the barn."

Parker left through the back door and stepped out on the porch as Trace Travis drove by in a Whiskey Gulch Ranch truck and parked in the barnyard next to another truck with a pallet of feed sacks in the bed.

Parker went down the porch steps and started across the yard toward his boss.

As Trace climbed out of the truck, Lily emerged from the barn with a smile. "You're just in time to lend a hand."

Trace nodded, opened his arms and engulfed her in a big hug. Then he kissed her, long and hard.

Finally, he set her on the ground, his arms around her waist.

"Wow," she said. "What was all that about?"

"Nothing. Everything." He smiled down at her. "I love you, Lily. I don't think I say it often enough."

She leaned up and kissed his lips. "You do. But I don't get tired of hearing it. I love you, too."

Parker stopped several yards from the tender scene, not comfortable interrupting, but anxious to speak with Trace.

Irish came out of the barn about that time and raised a hand. "Parker, is everything all right? I found your horse in his stall still saddled. I was just about to go looking for you."

Trace and Lily glanced from Irish to where Parker stood.

He'd completely forgotten Jasper in his hurry to get Abby warmed up.

"I had an issue come up and got sidetracked. I'll take care of my horse in a little bit."

Irish shook his head. "No worries. I already took care of him. Your tack is in the tack room, the horse has been brushed and is currently eating oats and hay. I'll turn him out to pasture when we're done unloading the truck."

"Thanks." Parker turned to Trace. "If you can spare a minute, I need to talk to you."

Lily stepped out of Trace's arms.

"Certainly. Here or in my office?" Trace strode toward him.

"In your office," Parker said and turned to walk alongside Trace toward the house.

"Did you find the break in the fence?" Trace asked as they climbed the porch steps together.

"No," Parker said. "I didn't make it that far."

Trace frowned as he led the way inside and down the hallway to his office. "What happened?" he asked as he held the door for Parker to enter.

Once Parker was inside and Trace closed the door, he started. "Brutus found a woman."

Trace's eyebrows shot up. "A woman? Where?"

"On the ranch, near the southern fence you wanted me to inspect," Parker said.

He gave Parker a crooked smile. "By woman, you mean human, not dog, right?" He settled in the chair behind his desk.

"Human."

Trace's smile faded. "Dead or alive?"

"Alive." Parker took a deep breath and launched into what had happened, pacing across the floor as he spoke. Minutes later, he stopped and faced Trace.

Trace whistled. "Hell of a first day on the job, huh?"

Parker nodded. "Not exactly what I was expecting to find on my first day."

"Why didn't you take her to the hospital? She could be suffering from hypothermia and hallucinations."

Parker still wanted to take her, but he'd promised her that he wouldn't. "She doesn't want anyone to know she's alive. Since none of the women knew who abducted them, Abby's afraid they would be able to identify her before she could identify them. She's also afraid that if she turns up alive, they'll hurry to get rid of the evidence and either make a hurried sale of the women, move them or kill them and hide the bodies."

Trace pushed hand through his hair. "They might have moved them already."

"I thought the same," Parker said. "Abby said she ran a long way without seeing any other lights. She also said it was raining hard when she left the house. It's possible she didn't see any other lights through the downpour."

"Yet, she ended up on Whiskey Gulch Ranch."

"Running barefoot all the way." Parker's jaw

clenched. The bastards who'd abducted her needed to die.

"I'll call the team to have dinner with us tonight. And, so you know, I had a meeting with the sheriff today. He asked for any help we could give him in finding a missing teen from a neighboring town."

"Abby said two of the women were teenagers."

Trace's eyes narrowed. "I'd like to get the sheriff involved."

"You can't. Abby couldn't have run through the entire county. Not at night, in the dark and rain. Which means the house where she and the other women were held could be fairly close. The men who abducted those women could live in the county. They could live in the town of Whiskey Gulch."

"From what you said, the women weren't all from around here."

"No. The teenage runaway was picked up in San Antonio. The college student was taken from a truck stop along the interstate between Whiskey Gulch and San Antonio. A young mother was picked up on the interstate when she stopped to change a flat tire. She even had children in the vehicle. They took her and left the children. The other teenager was taken after she got off a school bus a quarter mile from her house."

"Damn," Trace said. "Their families have to be worried sick."

"We can't let them know their loved ones are still alive," Parker said.

Trace's mouth set in a firm like. "Especially since we're not sure they are still alive, nor do we know where they are. All the more reason to get started on our search right away."

Parker nodded. "My thoughts exactly."

Trace picked up his cell phone. "I'll get the team together. We'll meet here, in my office, in forty-five minutes."

Parker nodded. "I want to go check on her again. She needs food and water."

"I'm sure my mother will fix her up." Trace selected a number and hit Send.

"I'd rather not announce her presence until everyone understands the implications of disclosing that she's here."

"Okay. But my mother and Lily know this house. It won't be long before they discover the extra guest." His attention focused on his phone. "Matt, I'm calling an emergency meeting in my office…as soon as possible. If you could contact Levi, I'll inform Becker… Roger. Out."

Parker left Trace's office and returned to the kitchen.

Rosalyn had finished putting away the groceries and had a stack of ham and cheese sandwiches on a platter on the counter.

"There you are," she said with a smile. "Help yourself to the sandwiches. There's a cup on the counter. I have tea and lemonade in the refrigerator, or I can make coffee."

"Water will be fine." He wasn't sure what Abby had been given to eat and drink during her incarceration. At this point, anything was better than nothing.

He wrapped two sandwiches in paper towels, filled the cup with water from the tap and left the kitchen.

He hurried up the stairs almost afraid he'd get to his room and find the bed empty and Abby Gibson nothing but a figment of his imagination.

Balancing the sandwiches on top of the cup, he reached for the door handle, took a deep breath and held it as he pushed the door open.

His gaze went right to the bed and he exhaled in relief.

Abby lay on her side, her arm draping over the side of the bed resting on Brutus's back.

Brutus rose, stretched and trotted over to Parker, sniffing the air, his gaze on the sandwiches.

"Don't worry, I'll give you some of mine." He closed the door and carried the cup and sandwiches to the bed and set them on the nightstand.

A cool breeze swept through the room.

Parker crossed to the French doors and closed them. He hadn't opened them before he left. Abby must have done it. After being locked in a cage in a dark attic for days, she probably needed to know she could open the doors and leave whenever she wanted. Still, the air in the room was too cool. If she wanted the doors opened again, he would do it for her.

When Parker turned back to the bed, Abby's eyes were open.

"Hey," he said. "Feel like eating something?"

She nodded, stretched and pushed to a sitting position. A shiver shook her frame. Abby pulled the comforter up over her chest.

Parker handed her a sandwich and moved the cup of water closer to her.

"Thank you," she said as she unwrapped the paper towel.

"You're welcome," he said as he took out the other sandwich and tore off a piece of bread for Brutus.

The dog sat three feet away, salivating.

"You'd think I never feed you." He tossed the bread into the air.

Brutus caught it before it hit the ground and swallowed it whole.

"You might try chewing next time." Parker tore off another piece and Brutus easily caught the offering again and chewed it before swallowing.

"That's more like it." Parker reached out and scratched behind Brutus's ear.

"You two have a special bond, don't you?" Abby took a small bite of her sandwich.

Parker nodded. "He and I helped each other through some dark times. Together, we help Jasper, as well."

"Jasper?" Abby asked over the sandwich in her hands.

"My horse."

"They mean a lot to you," she observed.

Parker nodded. "They do."

"Did you talk to your boss?"

"I did," Parker said and bit into his sandwich.

Abby captured his gazed and held it. "Well?"

Parker chewed the bite and swallowed before answering. "He's calling in the rest of the team."

She sighed. "I worry that the more people who know I'm alive and here, the more chance of it slipping out."

"The people on this ranch can be trusted."

"So you say." She stared down at the sandwich. "People can slip up and not even realize what they've done."

"In a perfect world, we'd enlist the help of everyone in the county to look for the women. But it's not a perfect world. And we need more eyes on the ground and in the air."

She set the food on the nightstand and picked up the cup of water and sipped. "When will they be here?"

Parker glanced at his watch. "Thirty minutes or less."

"I want to talk to them." Abby swung her legs over the side of the bed and reached for the brush next to the lamp on the nightstand. She dragged the brush through her hair, working the tangles. She stopped several times to rest.

Parker held out his hand.

Abby handed the brush to him.

"Turn around," he said.

She did, sitting cross-legged on the bed.

He eased the brush over her long blond hair, gently teasing the tangles loose.

"You know that if you go downstairs, the other members of the household will notice you," he reminded her.

"Then we'll have to make sure they're on board for keeping my secret." Her mouth pressed into a thin line. "It's all risky."

"We'll do our best." Parker smoothed the tangles and brushed Abby's hair straight back.

"Where did you learn to brush long hair?"

"Would it bother you if I said I once had long hair?" He grinned.

Abby's eyes rounded. "Of course not."

"Back as a freshman in high school, I was a bit of a rebel."

"And now?" she asked.

He chuckled. "The army worked it out of me and let me use it at the same time. It takes a rebel to pull off some of the missions we've been tasked with."

"Once a rebel, always a rebel?"

"Yes. But I can only go by my experience."

"And where did you learn to brush a woman's hair?"

"Like that?" he asked.

"Oh, yes," Abby said.

"I have two younger sisters. I helped get them ready for school in the mornings." Though all the tangles were gone, Parker continued to brush Abby's hair. "I even learned to French-braid. Mom never could get the hang of it. A friend of mine showed me how to do it. I practiced on my sisters until I got it right."

"You're an amazing man," Abby said. "And you can bush my hair as long as you like."

He continued for a few more minutes.

Her hair had dried and lay soft and straight around her shoulders, the light blond color a distinct contrast with the black T-shirt.

"I didn't know what I had when Brutus found you in the dirt."

"Yeah?" She turned to face him, her face clean of dirt and makeup, her lips a dusty rose and eyes light blue like a fresh spring sky. "I must have been a mess."

He frowned, far too aware of her in his T-shirt and shorts, so much of her legs bare. He needed to maintain focus on the issue, not how beautiful she was. "I never would have seen you if not for Brutus."

Abby reached down to scratch behind the pit bull's ears. "I'm lucky you both found me. Now, if only Brutus could sniff out the others, we'd make this go a whole lot faster."

"If anyone can find them, it's the Outriders."

She sighed. "I hope so. They're desperate to get home to their loved ones."

"And you?" he asked. "Are you desperate to get home to your loved ones?" This was the first time he'd considered that Abby might have someone else in her life. A husband, fiancé or significant other waiting for her to return.

"If you count my twenty-four fifth graders, I have twenty-four loved ones waiting for my return."

"No boyfriend?"

She snorted. "I teach fifth graders. I barely have time to grade all the students' papers."

Parker didn't want to admit to himself the relief he felt that she was single.

His gaze captured hers. "It takes a special person to teach. My mother was a teacher."

"Then you know how much work it is."

He nodded. "I do."

A knock sounded on the door.

Abby jumped, her eyes rounding.

Parker reached out to touch her leg. "It's okay."

"Parker," Irish's voice sounded on the other side of the door.

"Yeah?" Parker responded.

"Team's gathered," he said. "Trace wants us to meet in his office."

"Roger," Parker said. "I'll be right down." He stood and looked down at Abby seated on the side of the bed. He held out his hand. "Coming?"

She sighed and placed her hand in his.

He pulled her to her feet and into his arms.

She rested a hand against his chest and stared up into his eyes.

"Why is it that I've only just met you and already I want to kiss you."

A smile spread across her face. "What are you waiting for?"

"I don't want to take advantage. You've been through a lot."

She laughed. "Seriously?" Abby cupped both of his cheeks between her palms. "My feet hurt, I'm physically and emotionally exhausted, and afraid for the others I left behind. A kiss could only improve the day." She pressed her lips to his. "If you're the one doing the kissing. Please." Her lips took his, her tongue sweeping across his mouth.

He opened to her, his tongue caressing the length of hers.

When he finally broke away, he held her at arm's length and stared down into her eyes. "I don't know what that was all about, but damned if I don't want to do it again."

Chapter Six

Trace's entire team had gathered in his office. Trace sat behind the massive mahogany desk. Levi and Becker had each claimed one of the leather chairs. Irish perched on the edge of Trace's desk and Matt stood looking out the French doors.

Parker stood on the threshold, holding Abby's hand. He'd given her a pair of his sweatpants and socks. Everything she wore swamped her small frame. She'd walked gingerly on her bruised and damaged feet. With her shoulders back and her head held high, she entered the room, ready to go to work finding the women, her tight grip on Parker's hand due to determination, not fear.

"Gentlemen, this is Abby Gibson," Parker said. "Brutus discovered her this morning on the south end of the ranch."

The men rose from their seats as Abby entered the room.

Trace rounded the corner of his desk and took her hand. "Ms. Gibson, please, have a seat."

He led her to his office chair and held it while she eased onto the leather. Then he turned to the others. "Ms. Gibson needs our help. Our mission is time-sensitive and the lives of four women are at stake." He glanced down at Abby. "Do you want to tell them what's happened?"

She caught Parker's gaze and held it as she spoke. "For me, it started four days ago."

She detailed her abduction, holding herself together throughout the narrative all the way to her escape and subsequent race to freedom. "I managed to get out, but there are four other women being held against their will. I promised to get help." Abby looked around the room. "Parker said your group could help. I pray that's the case. Those women, two of whom are teens, have no other hope of being found. They'd been there longer than I had."

Trace nodded toward Abby. "The answer is yes. We will help." He faced his team.

Parker barely knew these men. Based on Trace's faith in them and the fact most of them had fought as Delta Force operatives, Parker would put his life in their hands and trust that they would do their best to find and free the women and bring their captors to justice.

"Time is critical," Trace said. "If they haven't already moved them, it's a high possibility they will... soon, unless they're convinced—" he waved a hand toward Abby "—that Ms. Gibson succumbed to her injuries before she had a chance to reveal their whereabouts. The women's lives and freedom depend on us keeping a lid on this. Y'all know the drill. Let's get to it."

"Yes, sir!" the men replied as one.

"Ms. Gibson," Trace started.

"Please," Abby stopped him. "Call me Abby. Only my fifth graders call me Ms. Gibson. Y'all don't look anything like fifth graders and it's throwing me off." She gave a crooked grin.

Trace nodded. "Abby escaped last night right about the time it started raining. She found her hiding space shortly after the rain stopped. Given she ended up on the south end of the ranch, she must've come through the break in the fence. She couldn't have traveled too far in her condition and under the circumstances, even with adrenaline pumping. We can create a grid of the area and start our search within a five-mile radius."

"We need to get a drone in the sky," Irish said.

Trace nodded. "You're right. We're on borrowed time. A ground search will take too long."

"I'll get it ready," said Matt.

"Parker and Abby, you'll need to work closely with Matt and Irish," Trace said.

Parker nodded.

"I'd like to get Dallas involved. She can research the names of the women abducted and see if there's a pattern that would help reveal the identities of their abductors."

"Who's Dallas?" Abby asked.

Trace's gaze met Parker's and then connected with Abby's. "Dallas is Levi's fiancée. She's a deputy sheriff in this county."

Abby shook her head. "No law enforcement. If word gets out—"

Levi held up his hand, stopping her words. "Dallas won't let that happen. None of us will."

Abby chewed on her lip as she glanced around the room at the men. "I'm not even comfortable with the number of people in this room, and you're asking me to let someone else in on it?" Her gaze landed on Parker.

He gave her a single nod. "They can be trusted," he said.

"And what about the deputy?" She held his gaze. "Do you know him?"

"Her," Levi corrected. "She's also prior military and knows the importance of keeping secrets."

"Those women are counting on me."

"And finding and rescuing them and taking down those responsible will be impossible by yourself," Trace said. "Let us help in the best manner we know how."

For a long moment, Abby stared around the room, a crease across her forehead. Finally, she sighed. "You're right. I can't do this by myself."

"And if they've moved them, it will be even more difficult to find them," Parker squeezed the hand he still held. He hated that she was so afraid and desperate. In his gut, he knew this team was her best bet.

"Okay," she finally said. "We need to hurry."

Trace turned to Matt. "Go get the drone."

Matt was already halfway across the room. "I'll be back in less than thirty minutes."

"Levi—" Trace started.

"I'll give Dallas a heads-up we need her to pay a visit to the ranch. She's on graveyard shift and sleeping right now. She could be out here later this evening to talk with Abby before she heads to work at midnight."

Trace glanced at his watch. "In the meantime, while we're waiting for Matt, the rest of us can pull up a satellite map for the surrounding area and see if we can narrow down the possibilities."

Trace turned back to Abby. "You realize my fiancée and mother live in this house. They'll have to know you're here."

She nodded.

"Could I bring them in and introduce them to you?" Trace asked.

"Okay," she said, holding onto Parker's hand.

He gave her a reassuring smile.

Trace left the room and returned a couple minutes later with three women.

Irish leaped to his feet and crossed to Tessa and pulled her into his arms. "Hey, babe."

She looked around the room, her gaze landing on Abby.

Rosalyn and Lily also looked to Abby.

"We have a guest?" Rosalyn asked.

Trace nodded. "Mom, Lily, Tessa, this is Abby Gibson. She needs our help and will be staying with us for a few days. No one else can know she's here. No one but the people in this room." He stared hard at the women. Then he explained what had happened. "So, we need to keep this to ourselves until we find those women."

"Why don't you call the sheriff and state police in to help?" Rosalyn asked. "Surely the more people you have looking, the quicker you'll find them?"

"Or they could move them or kill them and hide the bodies," Trace said. "We need to find them before that happens."

Rosalyn nodded. "Okay. My lips are sealed."

"And mine," Lily said.

"That goes for me, too," Tessa said. Her eyes narrowed as she studied Abby. "Are you sure you're all right? After what you've been through, a visit to a doctor would be a good idea."

Abby shook her head. "I'll be okay and even better when we find the others."

"At the very least, you should have Tessa look at the wounds on your feet and legs," Parker said. "She's a licensed nurse."

"Okay," she said. "If it's not too much trouble."

Tessa shook her head. "No trouble at all."

Rosalyn reached out a hand. "Come. I have a first aid kit in the master bathroom."

"And I'll find some clothes that fit you better," Lily said.

The women gathered around Abby and led her out of the office and down to the end of the hallway.

Parker stood in the doorway and watched them until they disappeared around a corner. He'd been with Abby since he'd found her in the dirt. That sense of responsibility for her welfare stuck with him, making him want to follow.

Trace clapped a hand on his shoulder. "They'll take good care of her."

"I know." Parker turned back to the room. "Let's look at those satellite maps. We need to find that house."

Trace nodded. "They could be targeting other women, looking for an opportunity to strike."

"Like Lily or Tessa." Parker's hands tightened into fists. "And no doubt they'll come after Abby if they find out she's still alive."

"We can't let any of that happen," Trace said. "Let's get to work."

As Rosalyn and Tessa led Abby away from Parker, her anxiety levels spiked. She almost stopped in her tracks and ran back.

When they turned the corner in the hallway, Abby glanced back.

Parker stood in the doorway of the office, his gaze on her.

Seeing him there, watching her, helped to calm her anxieties enough to allow her to continue with the women into the massive master suite.

"Those men need to pay for what they did to you," Rosalyn said. "I can't imagine how awful it must have been to be caged like an animal and then to have to run barefoot and half-naked." The older woman held her arm, walking her through the bedroom into the adjoining bathroom.

"I imagine your feet are like hamburger meat," Tessa said. "Texas hill country isn't kind on tender, bare feet."

Rosalyn pulled a white, tufted velvet stool from beneath a counter. "Sit here while I find the first aid kit." She gently pressed Abby onto the stool.

Tessa knelt on the floor in front of her.

Abby's cheeks heated. "You really don't have to do this."

"Yes, we do," Tessa said. "What kind of nurse would I be if I didn't?" She removed the big socks from Abby's feet and brought one up onto her knee and then the other, inspecting both carefully. "You did a good job cleaning them. Some antibiotic ointment wouldn't hurt and bandages for the deeper cuts when you're walking on them. Other than that, it'll take time for the wounds to heal and the bruises to fade."

Rosalyn opened a first aid kit and laid it on the floor beside Abby.

Tessa reached for an alcohol pad. "This will sting a little." She wiped the bottom of Abby's foot.

Abby sucked in a sharp breath at the burning sensation.

Rosalyn shook her head. "How on earth did you walk so far on bare feet?"

"I ran as long as I could. I guess my feet went

numb and I kept going. I was looking for lights from a house or business. Anywhere I could get help or use a phone."

"The south side of the ranch borders on several large tracts of land. I'm surprised you didn't run into any fences, but then some of those hills are rugged with little useful vegetation, usually dotted with cedar, cactus, scrubby live oak trees and very little grass," Rosalyn said.

Tessa applied antibiotic ointment and a large bandage to Abby's heels and the balls of her feet. "It would help if you slipped out of the sweatpants. I'm sure there are other wounds needing attention."

Abby stepped out of the sweats and shivered. She rubbed her hands up and down her arms, trying to get warm.

"Oh, sweetie, here." Rosalyn grabbed a fluffy white bathrobe off a hook behind the door and held it out to Abby.

She slipped her arms into the garment and wrapped it around her body. "I've never been so cold as I was last night, lying on the damp ground covered in wet leaves." Abby's teeth chattered from a combination of a chill and nervousness in front of the two women.

Tessa checked all the cuts and bruises, applied ointment and bandages where needed. She examined the raw skin around Abby's wrists and looked into Abby's eyes.

"Zip ties," Abby said.

Tessa shook her head. "We definitely need to find the men who did this and make sure they don't harm anyone else." She closed the kit and set it on the counter.

Lily sailed through the door carrying an armload of clothes. "Since I didn't know how long to plan for, I brought enough clothing for a week."

Abby shook her head. "I have my own clothes in my apartment in Boerne."

"I'm sure you do," Lily said. "But you're not going there until you're safe and those other women are safe as well. So you'll have to put up with my boring taste in clothes."

Abby's heart swelled at the outpouring of concern from Rosalyn, Tessa and Lily. Tears welled in her eyes. "Thank you. I don't know what I would have done if Parker and Brutus hadn't found me."

"You got out of a locked cage," Tessa said. "You'd have found a way to make things happen."

Like the men, the women had confidence in Abby's resilience. Abby believed everything she'd done so far had been performed out of pure desperation and a will to live.

Lily held up a pair of black leggings and a cream, cable-knit sweater. "This should keep you warm."

Abby reluctantly shed the robe and the black T-shirt. The robe for its warmth. The T-shirt because it was Parker's and smelled like him.

She quickly pulled the sweater over her head, wishing her bra was already dry.

The ladies gave her the courtesy of turning their

backs while Abby changed out of the T-shirt into the sweater.

She slipped out of the shorts and into the leggings. They weren't as warm as the sweats, but they fit her nicely and made her appear less like a vagabond. Still, she slipped the robe over the leggings and the sweater, basking in the warmth.

Rosalyn sat her back down on the stool and used her own brush to smooth Abby's hair.

When she was done, she stepped out of the way of the mirror and smiled at Abby's reflection. "There, that's better," Lily said. She leaned in and hugged Abby. "Don't worry. We'll get through this," she said. When she straightened, she held out a hand to Abby and pulled her to her feet.

Abby winced when her full weight came down on her damaged feel.

Tessa took her arm on one side. "You really need to stay off your feet until the wounds can heal." She looked at Abby, her eyebrows cocked. "You're not going to do that, are you?"

With a chuckle, Abby shook her head. "No. I can't sit around with my feet up when there are four women out there caged like animals. I'm ready to get started." And to get back to Parker. She only felt safe in his arms.

Chapter Seven

Parker, Trace, Irish and Becker skimmed through satellite images of the hill country south of the ranch, searching through the blurry images of tree crowns for the straight lines of rooftops.

Many of the places they found were so far from the ranch that they couldn't be from where Abby had originally escaped.

They also identified state highways and county roads they would need to use when they went in search of whatever house they found.

The sound of a truck engine made them all look up.

"That's Matt." Irish left his seat at the computer, unplugged the laptop from its docking station and carried it out of the office.

Trace, Becker and Parker followed.

Parker paused in the hallway.

At that moment, Abby, Rosalyn, Tessa and Lily came through the doorway.

Abby wore black leggings and a cream-colored sweater with a fluffy white bathrobe over it all.

He held out his hand.

She went to him, a smile curling the corners of her lips.

"Love the robe," he said. "Goes great with the rest of the outfit. Are you staying here, or coming with us?"

"With you," she said.

"I'll get Abby a coat." Lily hurried for the closet by the front door and returned with a Sherpa-lined jacket. "This should keep you warmer than the bathrobe."

Abby surrendered the robe and slipped her arms into the jacket. "Thank you for everything."

"I'm not sure we're going anywhere," Trace said, "but it'll be dark in less than an hour. We'll be less conspicuous then."

In the meantime, they recapped everything Abby had told them to make sure they hadn't missed anything. When the time came, everyone stepped out onto the porch as Matt climbed down from his truck. He reached into the back seat and withdrew a black drone and the handheld controls.

Irish joined Matt, laying the laptop on the hood of the truck.

"Battery fully charged?" Irish asked.

"Roger," Matt responded and laid the drone on the ground.

Trace stood nearby as Matt turned on the control

box and the drone and lifted the device into the air. After a few wobbly starts, Matt got the drone off the ground. He flew it up to ten feet and practiced moving side to side and forward and backward. Then he worked moving the drone up and down, landing it five times before finally going up to thirty feet in the air.

Matt directed the drone in a circle over the house, making a clockwise and then counterclockwise rotation. He did this three times around the house before sending the drone to circle the barn. Moving a little too fast, it almost crashed into the roof.

At the last moment, Matt made the drone climb higher, avoiding hitting the barn.

A collective gasp sounded from the spectators.

Parker shook his head. He reached for Abby's hand and squeezed it gently.

"The controls are very sensitive," Matt remarked.

Trace leaned over Matt's shoulder to view the screen and joysticks on the control box.

Matt circled the barn several times before bringing the drone back to land near their feet.

When it was on the ground, Matt wiped the sweat from his brow. "I need more practice."

Irish clicked the laptop keyboard and set up a livestream channel on his video app. He held out his hand. "Let me see the controls."

Matt handed over the control unit. Irish entered the URL website link on the control box, hit Enter and then looked to the laptop screen.

Irish swore, set the controls aside and keyed information on the laptop.

Once again, he played with the control box, entering data and clicking the enter key. This time an image of the gravel parking lot came into view. "Bingo! We're livestreaming."

Abby and the other women clapped their hands.

Matt reclaimed the control unit. "I need more practice here before I launch this over the hill country."

"And we need time with the drone in the air to understand what we're viewing," Irish said.

"Do all the practice you can this evening." Trace glanced at the sky. "Looks like we're in for some more rain. We'll have to wait until morning to fly it any distance." He glanced at his watch. "By the time we get to the south fence line, the sun will be setting. It'll be dark even sooner, with the clouds moving in. We can't risk losing the drone in the dark or the rain."

Abby's fingers tightened around Parker's. "That's another night those women will be held in captivity. Another night the men could use to move them."

"Hopefully, by keeping your whereabouts secret, they won't feel the need to do anything," Parker said.

"We can't do anything this late," Trace said. "Even if we rode out now on four-wheelers or horseback, we wouldn't cover enough ground to find anything. We'd barely get to the south fence line. We'll start out early tomorrow morning and be at the point where Parker found you by the time the sun comes up."

Abby's shoulders slumped. "I don't like it, but I understand." A cool breeze lifted her hair. She leaned against Parker, a shiver shaking her body.

Parker slipped an arm around her, sharing his own body warmth.

"I have a roast in the slow cooker," Rosalyn announced. "We can have supper on the table in thirty minutes with a little help."

"I can help." Parker glanced down at Abby. "Want to join me?"

She nodded "Anything to keep my mind off what those women are going through."

"Good," Parker said. "I can peel a mean potato and make chili, but that's about the extent of my culinary skills."

"Can you wield a knife?" Lily asked.

"In a fight, filleting fish and peeling potatoes, yes," Parker said.

"You two can cut the veggies for the salad," Lily said.

"I can help set the table," Becker volunteered.

"You're hired," Rosalyn said with a smile.

While Matt, Irish, Trace and Levi worked with the drone, the others entered the house.

In the kitchen, Rosalyn pulled out lettuce, tomatoes, carrots, purple onions and black olives from the refrigerator and pantry and set them out on the counter along with a large bowl, two cutting boards and a couple of sharp knives. "It's all yours."

Abby shed her jacket and hung it on a hook by the back door.

Parker grabbed the head of lettuce and started chopping.

Abby sliced the tomatoes.

They had the salad finished in ten minutes and set on the dining table with several bottles of various dressing options.

Abby filled glasses with ice from the ice maker on the refrigerator door. Parker carried them to the table and helped Becker finish setting out plates, cutlery and napkins.

Lily made iced tea and lemonade and set the pitchers on the table.

By the time Rosalyn carried the platter of roast beef, potatoes and carrots to the table, the sun had set.

Matt, Irish, Trace and Levi entered through the back door.

"Perfect timing," Rosalyn said. "We'll eat as soon as you boys wash up."

Everyone convened around the dining table.

Parker held Abby's chair and waited until she and the other women were seated before he claimed his seat next to Abby.

Lily, on the other side of Parker, handed him the platter of roast.

Parker scooped potatoes and carrots onto his plate and added a slice of roast beef. As he held the platter for Abby, he asked, "How are you holding up?"

She shrugged and took a small portion of the beef, a chunk of potato and a couple of carrots. Barely enough to call dinner. "I'm eating hot food while the other women are still captive and lucky if they get cold sandwiches once a day. They barely gave us food and water. I was so hungry, but the thought of eating while they're still suffering…"

"Think of it this way," Parker said. "You need to keep up your strength. Food is fuel for your body. Without it, you won't be of much use in finding them."

She nodded. "I know. I just feel like I wasted today. I should have been out looking for them, not sleeping."

He reached for her hand. "You needed the rest. After you raced through the storm last night and slept on the cold, wet ground, you're lucky to be alive."

She didn't look convinced.

Her melancholy made Parker want to hold her close and reassure her even more.

"Yoo-hoo!" A female voice called out from the front of the house. "Where is everyone?"

"That'll be Dallas." Levi rose from the table with a smile and called out, "We're in the dining room."

A woman wearing the tan-shirt-and-black-trouser uniform of the county sheriff's department stepped into the dining room with a grin. "Something smells really good," she said.

"Dallas," Rosalyn said with a welcoming smile. "So glad you could join us."

"I was getting ready for my shift when Levi texted saying you had one of your pot roasts cooking. I couldn't miss out." She glanced around the table, an eyebrow cocked. "That is, if there's enough for everyone."

Rosalyn waved a hand toward the empty chair beside Levi. "There's always enough. I always cook more than we'll need so we can snack on it later. Take a seat."

Levi held a chair for her. Once Dallas had taken her seat, Levi rested a hand on her shoulder, leaned forward and pressed a kiss to her temple. "Hey."

She covered his hand on her shoulder and looked up at him. "Hey."

Levi sat beside her and handed her the platter of food.

Dallas scooped a generous portion onto her plate and looked around the table. "Levi tells me I need to talk with the new guy and his gal." Her gaze landed on Parker and moved to Abby.

"Dallas," Trace said, waving toward Parker. "This is my newest Outrider, Parker Shaw."

Dallas nodded toward Parker. "Prior military?"

Parker nodded. "Army Delta Force."

"Thank you for your service," Dallas said.

"Dallas is prior army as well."

"What MOS?" Parker asked.

"31Bravo, Military Police." Dallas glanced down at her law enforcement uniform and shrugged. "Surprised?"

"Thank you for your service." Parker turned to Abby. "This is Abby Gibson."

Dallas nodded. "Are you prior service as well?"

Abby shook her head. "I'm a fifth grade teacher in Boerne."

Dallas's brow puckered. "Visiting here in Whiskey Gulch?"

"Not exactly," Abby said.

Dallas's frown deepened. "Abby Gibson. The name sounds familiar."

Levi leaned close to Dallas. "Abby's the reason why I wanted you to stop by the ranch before you went on duty tonight."

Dallas's gaze met Abby's. "What's the story?" She speared a bite of roast and popped it into her mouth as she listened to Abby's recounting of her abduction, the others in captivity and her subsequent escape.

Dallas's frown cleared. "That's where I heard your name. We had a BOLO come across from Kerrville PD about a late model silver Toyota Prius, the vehicle of a missing woman believed to have been abducted from a rest area near there."

"That would be me." Abby sighed.

Dallas pulled a pad and pen from her front pocket. "I'll need the names of the others."

Abby gave her what she knew. "Cara Jo Noble, Valentina Ramirez, Laura Owens and Rachel Pratt. From what I could gather, they planned to sell us."

Dallas frowned. "I recognize a few of those names

from Amber alerts. Can you describe any of the men involved?"

Abby shook her head. "No. They all wore ski masks. Cara Jo and Valentina described the man who abducted them as young, blond, nice-looking and approachable. He lured them in, asking for directions, then snatched them."

"I work the graveyard shift," Dallas said. "I usually patrol. I might be able to get some information from the computer on my unit, but I'll take my breaks at the office and do some more snooping on the main computers and databases." She glanced at Levi. "The Rangers should have pulled the cameras at the truck stop where Laura Owens was abducted. I'll see if I can get more info. I have a friend who might be able to help."

Abby leaned forward. "Dallas, I don't want anyone to know I'm here. I'd rather the men who kidnapped me think I died in that storm. It might buy some time before they move the other women."

"If I were them and one of my prisoners escaped," Dallas said, "I'd have moved the others immediately."

Parker agreed with Dallas but didn't voice his agreement. "At the very least, if we find the house they were held in, we might find some clues as to who is orchestrating these abductions and human trafficking."

Dallas nodded. "If they have moved, perhaps they were in such a rush they left behind clues or evidence as to who they are or where they're heading. I'm not sure how much I can delve into the case without letting my department know I'm accessing the information. But I'll do the best I can."

Abby gave her a weak smile. "Thank you."

Parker drew in a deep breath. "Since Abby ended up here on the ranch, we have to assume the men who did this are from around here or are staying close by. We don't know who they are. They could be anyone. We can't be too careful."

"Although my instinct is to remain hidden, it might help for me to be out in the nearby community." Abby wrapped her arms around her middle. "I might recognize one of them by voice."

"They would want to do away with the escapee." Dallas leveled a glance at Abby. "If you're out and about in Whiskey Gulch, you will want to wear some kind of disguise."

"I can fix you up with a disguise," Lily said. "My mother left me all her costumes. I'm sure I have a wig or two you could use. Add some big sunglasses, we can make you look completely different from the fifth grade teacher they snatched."

Parker gave her a puzzled look.

Lily shrugged. "My mother was a stripper. A story for another time. She had a whole trove of wigs and costumes. At least you won't have to hole up at the ranch if you can get out and about as Sissy Bling, or Lala Swoon." She grimaced. "Again, my mother went by a number of different stage names over the years."

"Lala Swoon?" Abby smiled. "I like it. And I've always wanted dark hair."

"I have the prettiest long, black wig," Lily said. "You'll look amazing in it."

"I thought you'd gotten rid of most of those old costumes," Trace said.

Lily gave him a sexy side-eye. "I kept a few of my favorites. You never know when I might take up the trade."

Trace's eyebrows dipped low. "The hell you will."

"I could give a private performance," Lily said, batting her eyelashes.

Trace's frown deepened.

Lily laughed. "Oh, don't be so stuffy." She turned to Abby. "We'll get you fixed up in case you want to go to town."

"Right now, I want to go back out to where Parker found me and retrace my footsteps."

"You were running in the dark, in a rainstorm," Parker said. "Your footsteps will have been washed away."

"And you might not have run in a straight line," Trace said. "It's highly unlikely. The drone is going to be our best bet. I'm also checking with a friend of mine to see if we can get a helicopter in the air if the drone doesn't work out."

"Wouldn't the noise warn them?" Abby asked, her brow furrowing.

"We need a backup plan if the drone doesn't help us find the house," Trace said.

FREE BOOKS GIVEAWAY

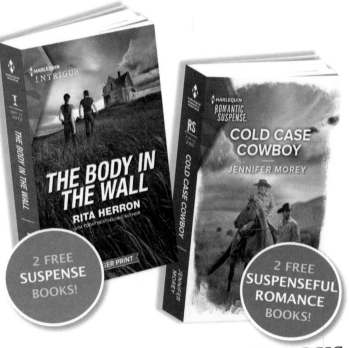

2 FREE SUSPENSE BOOKS!

2 FREE SUSPENSEFUL ROMANCE BOOKS!

GET UP TO FOUR FREE BOOKS & TWO FREE GIFTS WORTH OVER $20!

We pay for everything!

See Details Inside

Complete the survey below and return it today to receive up to 4 FREE BOOKS and FREE GIFTS guaranteed!

FREE BOOKS GIVEAWAY
Reader Survey

1	**2**	**3**
Do you prefer stories with suspensful storylines?	Do you share your favorite books with friends?	Do you often choose to read instead of watching TV?
◯ YES ◯ NO	◯ YES ◯ NO	◯ YES ◯ NO

YES! Please send me my Free Rewards, consisting of **2 Free Books from each series I select** and **Free Mystery Gifts**. I understand that I am under no obligation to buy anything, no purchase necessary see terms and conditions for details.

❑ **Harlequin® Romantic Suspense** (240/340 HDL GRRU)
❑ **Harlequin Intrigue® Larger-Print** (199/399 HDL GRRU)
❑ **Try Both** (240/340 & 199/399 HDL GRR6)

FIRST NAME   LAST NAME

ADDRESS

APT.#   CITY

STATE/PROV.   ZIP/POSTAL CODE

EMAIL ❑ Please check this box if you would like to receive newsletters and promotional emails from Harlequin Enterprises ULC and its affiliates. You can unsubscribe anytime.

HI/HRS-122-FBG22

◊HARLEQUIN Reader Service —Terms and Conditions:

BUSINESS REPLY MAIL
FIRST-CLASS MAIL   PERMIT NO. 717   BUFFALO, NY

POSTAGE WILL BE PAID BY ADDRESSEE

HARLEQUIN READER SERVICE
PO BOX 1341
BUFFALO NY 14240-8571

NO POSTAGE
NECESSARY
IF MAILED
IN THE
UNITED STATES

Dallas shook her head. "If we could get the DPS in on this, we might find them sooner. They're already looking for you and the other missing women."

"They'll move them," Abby said, shaking her head. "Or kill them and hide the bodies."

"I feel like I'm concealing key information." Dallas held up a hand. "Then again, we don't know where they are, so we aren't really." She finished her meal and pushed back from the table, collected her plate and glass and carried them into the kitchen.

One by one, the others followed, until the table was clear.

Dallas hugged Trace's mother. "Rosalyn, thank you for a wonderful meal. I think I'll get to work early and do some digging around for information about the abductions and also see if there are any felons living in the area we should be watching."

"Thank you, Dallas," Abby said. "For helping us find them, and for keeping quiet about me."

Dallas gave her a crooked smile. "I'll work through some of my contacts to keep this on the down low. I'll do the best I can." She pointed at Abby. "Stay safe."

"I'll make sure she does," Parker said.

Dallas nodded. "Nice to meet the new Outrider. Welcome to Whiskey Gulch. I promise we're not all bad here."

"I'm going to follow Dallas into town and head to our place for the night," Levi said. "Do you need me here in the morning?"

"No," Trace said. "But be on standby in case we find the house. We might need you for backup."

"Roger." Levi lifted his chin toward Rosalyn. "Thanks for supper, ma'am." He walked Dallas out to her vehicle. A few minutes later, Parker heard the sound of their engines as they left the yard and headed to town.

"Do you need help cleaning up?" Tessa asked.

Rosalyn shook her head. "We can manage."

"Okay, then. We need to get going," Tessa said. "I have to be up for an early shift in the morning."

Irish slipped an arm around Tessa's waist. "I'll be back before dawn." He caught Abby's glance. "We'll find them."

"Thank you for your help," Abby said.

Irish and Tessa left.

Abby looked around at the dishes on the counter in the kitchen. "I'll do the dishes," she said.

"Don't be silly." Rosalyn waved her hand. "You're a guest."

Abby shook her head. "An uninvited guest. It's the least I can do to repay your kindness."

Parker piled plates together and stacked them by the sink. "If you wash, I'll dry."

"Deal," she said and filled one side of the sink with soapy water.

"You know, we're pretty modern here," Rosalyn said. "We have a dishwasher."

"And I plan to use it," Abby said with a grin. "I'll wash the dishes by hand."

"Then I'm going to grab a beer and step outside to enjoy the evening," Rosalyn said. "Nothing is better than the smell of freshly washed earth after a rain." She grabbed a beer from the refrigerator, unscrewed the cap and handed it to Trace.

"Thanks," he took it and handed it to Lily. Then he got out two more bottles from the refrigerator, twisted off the caps and handed one to his mother. "Dinner was great. Thanks."

"You're welcome," Rosalyn slipped an arm around her son's waist as they walked out the back door onto the porch.

Parker liked that Trace was a man who cared about his family and cared about the men with whom he'd served.

He helped Abby rinse and load the dishes into the dishwasher. Then while she washed, he dried the dishes and the slow cooker.

Brutus found a rug to curl up on and napped while the humans worked.

Parker liked working alongside Abby. She didn't say much, and he didn't feel like he had to make conversation. They worked in a comfortable silence.

When he bumped into her on occasion, electric jolts zipped through his body, shocking him with the flame of desire quickly building. He'd found her dirty, nearly naked and desperate, climbing out of what amounted to a shallow grave. Yet, she stood beside him hours later, willing to work as repayment for her hostess's hospitality. That she was willing to go back to where she'd been held captive showed courage and a caring heart.

He liked this woman and wanted to get to know her better.

She emptied and rinsed the sink and hung the dishtowel on the oven handle.

"Are you heading to bed?" he asked.

She shook her head. "I'd like to spend some time outside, if that's all right. It's not often I get to be where city lights don't shine and hide the stars. And after being stuck inside an attic for days…"

He nodded. "You want to be in the open without walls around you."

"Exactly."

"Would you like a beer?" he asked.

She nodded. "That would be nice."

He claimed two from the refrigerator, opened them and handed her one. Then he raised his bottle and tapped hers. "To finding them quickly."

Abby nodded and tipped her bottle up, downing a long swallow. She held up her beer. "To heroes who rescue damsels in distress."

Brutus chose that moment to lean against her legs.

Abby laughed. "Yes, Brutus, that means you, too."

"He's the real hero," Parker said. "He found you and stood guard against the feral hogs."

She raised her eyebrows. "And if you hadn't swept me off my feet when you did, that herd of hogs would have overwhelmed poor Brutus and had us both for lunch." Abby touched his bottle with hers again. "To hero teams who rescue damsels in distress."

"I'll drink to that." He tipped his bottle back and swallowed. "Let's go look at some stars. I'm feeling the walls closing in around me." He grabbed her jacket from the hook by the door and helped her into it. Once she had it zipped, he held out his hand.

Abby curled her fingers around his and leaned into him as they stepped out onto the porch.

She fit nicely against his side, like she belonged there. Having saved her life really had left an impression and an obligation with him. More than an obligation or duty. He was *compelled* to continue protecting her.

Whether she liked it or not, she was stuck with him.

Chapter Eight

Cool night air felt good against Abby's cheeks. She lifted her face to the gentle breeze, glad for the jacket to keep her body warm.

Other than the light shining through the window in the kitchen, no other lights had been turned on. The stars glowed brightly enough she could see all the way past the barn to where Parker's horse, Jasper, grazed in the field.

"We were about to send a search party into the house to see what was keeping you two." Lily asked from where she perched on the porch rail with Trace beside her.

"Sorry. We got carried away talking," Abby said.

"Thank you for cleaning the kitchen," Rosalyn said from her seat on the porch swing. "We're glad you joined us. We couldn't ask for better weather after last night's storm."

"I, for one, am grateful for last night's storm," Lily said.

"Me, too," Abby murmured softly.

"We needed the rain," Trace said. "Another week without it, along with the cooler weather, and the grass would've died, and we'd have to feed the animals hay sooner."

"That little bit of rain will buy us another week or two of grazing," Lily said.

Parker led Abby down the steps and out into the yard before he stopped and looked up at the sky.

Abby tipped her head back and stared at the bright stars, thankful to be outside where she could stretch her arms and legs and breathe clear, crisp air.

"I'm sorry we didn't make any more progress toward finding the others today," Trace said.

"I am, too," Abby said. "I hope they're okay and can hold out a little longer until we can get to them."

"We all hope the same," Lily said. "I can't imagine what their families are going through. I'd be tempted to tell them you know they're alive."

"I thought the same." Abby shook her head. "But they're better off not knowing. What if we don't get there in time? If they're moved to another location or worse? We'd have given their families hope only to be crushed again."

"Good point," Rosalyn said. "It must have been horrible being trapped in cages. I'm amazed you were able to break free."

"That took a great deal of courage," Trace said.

Abby shook her head. "Desperation. By day three, I was starting to lose hope that we were ever going to be rescued. I figured it was up to us. Then the storm came and the thunder helped drown out the noise I made. So, yes, I was grateful for last night's storm. And though I can't retrace my footsteps, neither can anyone track them here."

Rosalyn pushed to her feet. "I'm headed for a shower and bed. Tomorrow will be a busy day for us all. While you guys are flying drones, I have the farrier coming to work on the horses' hooves. I would reschedule, but he's booked out two months in advance. Once I get the horses into the stalls, I'll come help however I can."

"We shouldn't need you out there," Trace said. "We're going to be looking at a computer screen and tracking against the map. When we find a building, we'll be back to the house and going around by road. My team will handle that. We don't know what we'll be up against."

Rosalyn nodded. "I'll be up early to make drinks and sandwiches to take with you. And I'll have something ready for supper at the end of the day."

"You don't have to cook for us." Trace walked over to his mother and kissed the top of her head. "We can get dinner in town."

"Whatever you decide, let me know early enough so I don't make up a big meal if no one will be here to eat it."

"Plan on us eating out. If we don't, we're old enough to make our own sandwiches." He hugged his mother. "Get some sleep. You know I love you."

She patted her son's cheek. "I know. And I love

you, too." She leaned up on her toes and kissed his cheek. "Be careful tomorrow.

"Promise," Trace said. "Good night."

"Good night, everyone," Rosalyn entered the house, closing the door softly behind her.

"I'm tired as well," Lily said. "I'm calling it a night." She looked up into her fiancé's eyes. "Coming?"

He smiled down at her. "You bet." Trace turned to Parker and Abby. "If you need anything, help yourself, or don't hesitate to ask. And lock the back door behind you when you come in. I'll get the rest."

Parker nodded. "We'll lock up."

Lily took Trace's hand and led him through the back door into the kitchen.

Finally alone, Abby wrapped her arms around herself and looked out at the endless heaven of stars.

They were at once reassuring in their consistent appearance every night and frightening with the sheer vastness of their expanse. She could easily feel small and insignificant, a tiny speck in the universe.

Abby moved closer to Parker. He was her rock in the troubled flow of her existence. With him, she felt grounded and secure. Away from her, she was quickly consumed by a tsunami of emotions and fear.

Parker slipped an arm around her shoulders and pulled her close. "I'm here for you," he said softly.

"How did you know I needed you to be?" she whispered.

He shrugged. "I don't know. I just felt it."

She leaned into him. "Thank you for being here with me. I don't think I could do this without you."

He shook his head. "You could. And you did up to the point Brutus found you."

"Still, I was close to going to sleep and never waking up. I've never felt that cold inside and out." She shivered.

His arm tightened around her. "Are you ready to go in? The temp is dropping."

Abby nodded. "I guess we need to get some rest. Tomorrow is going to be stressful."

"Yes, it will be." He turned her around and headed up the stairs onto the porch.

He held the door for her as she entered.

Brutus slipped in behind her.

Parker followed, pulled the door closed behind them and twisted the lock to engage the dead bolt.

"I asked Lily to let you sleep in the room next to mine," Parker said as they climbed the stairs to the second floor.

"Thank you."

"If you have a nightmare, I'll be right next door."

"I'll try not to wake you," she said.

"That's not what I meant," he reached for her hand. "I'll be there when you need me. I'm a light sleeper. All you have to do is call out my name."

Her cheeks heated. She'd always been an independent woman who didn't let much scare her. But having been forcefully taken and held against her will with no easy way out, her confidence had taken a huge hit. "Thank you. I'll keep that in mind."

Parker passed the room he'd brought Abby to earlier that day and moved on to the next one beside it. He opened the door and stood back, waiting for Abby to enter.

She stepped through and looked around. Like the other rooms in the house, it was open and airy, with French doors leading out onto the same upper deck as the room Parker was staying in.

Knowing she could get to him through two different doors helped somewhat to alleviate her anxiety over being left alone.

Brutus slipped past her and lay on the rug at the end of the bed.

Parker stepped into the room, turned her around and stared down into her eyes. "Are you going to be all right?"

She gave him a weak smile, her brave facade slipping as a lump formed in her throat. Unable to push words past that lump, she nodded, refusing to meet his gaze.

Parker cupped her cheeks in both hands and tipped her chin up, his gaze connecting with hers. "It's okay to be scared. And it's okay to admit it. There's no shame in it." He bent to touch his lips to her forehead.

Abby leaned into that kiss. The next thing she knew, she'd wrapped her arms around his waist and pressed her forehead to his chest. "I'm scared."

"Do you want me and Brutus to stay with you until you go to sleep?" he asked softly.

She hated her weakness but hated even more being left alone. Abby nodded. "Please."

Parker kicked the door shut behind him. "Go. Get ready for bed. I'll be right here."

She looked up into his eyes for confirmation.

He stood firm, meeting and holding her gaze.

Finally, she backed away, her arms falling to her sides.

When she turned away, her anxiety ramped up, her chest tightened, and she almost flung herself back into his arms.

Abby stood for a moment, breathing in and out until she could move forward, away from Parker.

The stack of clothes Lily had loaned her were lying on the bed. Among them was a nightgown, a hairbrush, a new toothbrush and a small tube of toothpaste. Abby gathered the nightgown and toiletries and headed into the adjoining bathroom. She glanced back at Parker before she closed the door between them.

Quickly, she stripped out of the coat, sweater, trouser and shoes and slipped the nightgown over her head. She opened the package with the toothbrush, spread toothpaste on the bristles and ran it beneath the water.

She brushed her teeth for a long time. After three days without a brush and toothbrush, she'd never take them for granted again.

Once she'd finished brushing her teeth, she ran the brush through her hair, smoothing the tangles until it fell softly around her shoulders.

She studied her reflection in the mirror, seeing a stranger, remembering how she'd felt when she'd been forced to stand in front of a potential buyer like cattle at an auction. Even wearing the school T-shirt, she'd felt naked and dirty, and completely helpless to change a thing as long as the captor threatened her with the cattle prod.

Now, her body, hair and teeth were clean. The gown fell to the middle of her thighs, the snow-white fabric a semi-sheer material with lace embellishments along the plunging neckline.

She left the bathroom, intent on throwing herself in the bed and pulling the blanket up to her chin to hide her body.

She'd only taken two steps when she came to a halt.

Parker stood with his back to her, giving her the privacy she needed to make it to the bed without embarrassment or a panic attack.

Her heart swelled and tears welled in her eyes. She tiptoed to the bed, pulled back the comforter and slid between the sheets.

How had she been so lucky as to be rescued by a man who was not only strong and handsome, but a gentleman who obviously sensed her panic and made it easy on her by giving her the space she needed.

"You can turn around," she said softly, pulling the sheet up to her chin.

When he did, his brow puckered as he studied her face. "Feel better?"

She nodded. "I think I scrubbed a layer of enamel off my teeth."

"I know what it means to have access to a toothbrush after days in the combat." He smiled. "It makes you appreciate good dental care."

She smiled. "That's just what I was thinking."

He walked over to a high-backed, floral-patterned chair positioned close to the French doors. "Do you mind if I sit?"

She turned on her side and craned her neck to see him where he stood by the chair. "Could you bring the chair closer before you do? I can't see you easily over there."

He lifted the fancy chair and carried it over to set it down gently next to the bed. "Better?"

She smiled. "Yes, thank you."

He went to the bathroom, turned on the light and closed the door but for a crack. Then he turned off the light on the nightstand, plunging the room into shadows, with only a wedge of light from the bathroom.

"Is that enough light?" he asked.

She nodded. "Thank you for leaving the light on in the bathroom. We spent much of our time in the dark with only our voices to remind us we weren't alone."

Parker lowered himself into the flowery chair, his hands on the armrests. "You should try to sleep. Tomorrow will be a long day."

She nodded and closed her eyes. That panicky feeling spiked and her pulse took off at a gallop. She opened her eyes. When her gaze landed on the man in the chair next to her bed, her pulse slowed back to normal.

He'd closed his eyes and leaned his head back against the chair cushion. He was a handsome man with dark hair and darker eyes. One of those dark eyes opened. "You're not sleeping."

"I will. But I'd rather fall asleep with my eyes open."

He frowned. "That's hard to do."

She shrugged. "Closing them makes me anxious. I feel like I'm back in the dark attic. I'm sure I'll go to sleep eventually. But don't let me keep you awake."

His lips quirked upward. "Right." He shifted in the chair, clearly uncomfortable. It didn't even lean back or allow him to put his feet up.

Guilt tugged at Abby's belly. "You can't be comfortable in that chair."

"I've slept in worse," he said, crossing his arms over his chest and one ankle over the other, stretching his legs out in front of him. Both eyes closed.

Abby watched for a long while before she said, "You don't have to stay. I'll be okay."

"I told you I'd stay until you fell asleep," he said with his eyes closed.

"What if I don't go to sleep?" she asked. "You can't sit in that chair all night.

"I can, if I need to," he said. "Now hush and sleep."

She lay for another couple of minutes, shaking her head. "You can't sleep like that," she burst out. "You need rest for tomorrow even more than I do. Go to your room and sleep."

He chuckled and looked at her through slitted eyes. "Is that how you talk to your fifth graders?"

"No. They listen to me and do as I say." She frowned. "Please. I can't feel right about you sleeping in that chair all night."

"I'll be fine. Besides, sleep is overrated." He smirked. "Or so my old commander tried to tell me."

"If you won't go to your room, at least lie down on the bed with me. I won't allow you to pretend to sleep in that chair for another minute. I'm already bearing the guilt of leaving those women. I won't feel right if something happens to you tomorrow because you're too exhausted to think straight."

He sat up, his brow furrowing. "I'm not going to my room."

Abby scooted to one side of the bed and patted the empty space with her hand. "Lie down on the bed."

He shook his head with a smirking half smile. "We're practically strangers," he said. "It wouldn't be right."

"I don't give a flying flip if it's right. What's wrong is you sleeping in that horrible chair." She gave him her best stern-teacher stare. "Now, get over here, or go to your own room."

His eyes narrowed. "I can't get into the bed with you."

"Why not?" Her brow twisted. "Are you married or something?"

"Something," he said.

"Oh. You have a significant other?"

"No, the something is that I'm attracted to you. Getting in a bed with you, and not touching you, will lead to a whole lot more hurt than sitting up all night in this chair." He leaned his head back again and closed his eyes. "Now, stay awake or go to sleep, but be quiet whatever you do. I'm trying to catch some z's."

Abby lay still, her pulse racing for an entirely different reason now.

"You're attracted to me?" she whispered, her heart pounding so hard she was sure he could hear it from where he sat in his chair.

"Of course, I am." His forehead creased. "But don't worry. I won't act on it. You're safe with me."

Her blood burned through her veins and swirled low in her belly, coiling around her core. "What if I want you to touch me?" she asked.

His eyes shot open and then narrowed. "You're scared and not thinking straight. Understandable after the trauma you've experienced. But I'm not going to take advantage of your vulnerable condition. You deserve better."

"What makes you think you touching me wouldn't make things better?" She drew in a deep breath and let it out. "I *want* you to touch me. I'm not confused or just trying to use you for comfort, although you do give me that."

Parker's hands tightened on the armrests of the awful chair. "What kind of jerk would I be to take advantage of you when you've been through so much over the last four days?"

"You'd be the best kind of jerk," she said with a wicked smile. The more she thought about lying naked with Parker, the better she liked the idea.

"I'm not going to do it," Parker said as if reading her mind. "Your sensitivities are heightened. You may regret it later and wind up feeling worse than you do now. I can't let that happen."

"I'm willing to take that risk," she said.

"We're strangers. Why push this?"

"Why not? I don't want to be alone."

"So, you'll sleep with a perfect stranger? What if I were a serial killer?"

"You were properly vetted before you were asked to join this expedition. I'm convinced you aren't a serial killer," she said. "And last but not least, I'm on birth control and I'm clean, no STDs. Any other concerns?" She cocked an eyebrow and challenged him with a stare.

"I don't like being coerced into doing something," he grumbled.

"Didn't you just say you were attracted to me?" she demanded.

"I might have." Ruddy red color rose up Parker's neck into his cheeks. "And believe me it's easier to stop before you get started."

Abby sat up in the bed and crossed her arms of her chest like Parker. "Are you going to get into this bed?"

He shook his head. "No."

She stared at him with her lips pressed tightly together. "Fine." Abby turned her back to him, pulled the comforter up over her shoulders and forced herself to count freaking sheep. At eighty she gave up.

As fast as her heart was beating, she wouldn't go to sleep anytime soon.

She lay staring at the other side of the room, tired beyond caring.

The man was attracted to her and she couldn't even take advantage of that.

Right then, she needed the workout, and the closeness sex would provide. Then maybe she could fall asleep.

To hell with him.

She forced her eyes closed, pushed back her desire for the stubborn man and willed herself to calm and ultimately sleep.

Chapter Nine

Parker sat as still as he could until Abby's breathing grew deeper and slower. Finally, she was asleep.

He stood and adjusted himself in the tight confines of his jeans.

Yes, the woman made him hot all over. No, he didn't have to act on it. Yes, he wanted to make love to her more than he wanted to breathe.

But she wasn't ready for a man to force his attentions on her. It might trigger her into a panic attack.

Parker paced across the room. Abby had been right about one thing. He could never sleep sitting up in that chair. At the other end of the room, he spun and stared at the bed and the woman in it.

All he'd had to do was agree with her, climb into the bed and make love to her. He'd be satisfied and she'd be…what? Satisfied enough to sleep? Or even more traumatized?

Parker had seen panic in her eyes several times. Mostly at the idea of being alone.

His eyes narrowed. Not at being alone so much as

being without him. When she'd been led away by the women, she'd looked back for him. She hadn't been alone and wasn't going to be left alone in a room. Abby had wanted to be with him.

But was that purely a distraction so she didn't have to deal with her situation or was she genuinely attracted to him? Was it that she wanted to be with the man who'd saved her? Was it that she felt safe only with him?

He crossed the room and settled on the edge of the chair, his hands clasped between his knees. Why had he been so adamant about not lying in bed with her?

He knew the answer. Because she might have wanted him to make love to her out of some reaction to having no control over her life for the days she'd been held hostage. By making love with him, she had the control.

And when it was over, she would've regained control and would no longer need him.

Was that what he was worried about? If he made love to her, he might fall even more in love with her. And after she got over the trauma of her abduction, she'd no longer need him. By then, he'd be stupidly head over heels and left brokenhearted.

No. He'd made the right decision. He was better off not getting involved.

Abby rolled onto her back, her forehead dented in a deep frown, her eyes squeezed shut.

Parker could see the pulse at the base of her throat beating fast and furious.

Abby's fists clenched and her head moved side to side. "No," she murmured. "Lemme go."

Parker's chest squeezed tight.

She was in the middle of another nightmare.

He waited, hoping it would subside.

Her head rocked back and forth on the pillow. She drew her knees up to her chest and whimpered, tears flowing down her cheeks.

That was it. Parker could stand a lot, but the tears were his undoing.

He kicked off his shoes, pulled back the comforter and slid between the sheets next to Abby.

Her feet kicked out, again and again.

By now, soft sobs racked her body, the tears continuing to flow.

Parker slipped an arm beneath her and pulled her close. "Abby, honey. Wake up."

She pushed against him, fighting his hold on her.

"Abby, it's me, Parker. You're having a bad dream. Please sweetheart, wake up." He stroked her cheek, tucked a damp strand of hair behind her ear and kissed away her tears. All the while, he spoke to her in deep, soothing tones. "Abby, look at me. See me. It's Parker. I'm here. You're with me. You're going to be all right. Wake up."

Brutus rose from the rug at the end of the bed and came around to the side next to Parker and laid his chin on the mattress, his eyes wide and soulful.

When Abby whimpered again, Brutus whined.

"Abby, wake up," Parker said. "Brutus is worried about you."

Brutus whined again and laid a paw on the mattress.

"It's okay, Abby. Brutus and I have your back. We won't let anything bad happen to you." He held her close, rocking her in his arms.

Her eyes fluttered open and stared up into his. "Parker?"

"Yeah, baby. I'm here."

She looked around at the room, her eyes wide, her body tensing.

"You're safe, sweetheart. You're with me and Brutus at the Whiskey Gulch Ranch."

She sagged in his arms. "I thought I was back there."

"You're not. You're here with me."

She turned on her side and rested her cheek and her hand on his chest. "I thought you didn't want to get in bed with me," she said, her voice low and sexy as hell.

"I told you I was attracted to you." He touched his lips to her forehead. "You're beautiful, smart and brave. How could I resist?"

Her fingers settled on a button on his shirt. "I don't understand."

"What don't you understand?"

"If you're so attracted to me, why are you wearing so many clothes?" She flicked the button through the hole and moved to the next one, loosening it and then moved to the next.

He started to put his hand over hers and stop her journey down that path. But he didn't. Why fight it? She wanted him. He wanted her. What was the worst that could happen?

He was falling in love with this amazing woman.

He was a man used to taking risks with his life. But not with his heart.

He wasn't on active duty. He wouldn't be deployed by the army to some hostile hot spot where he could be surrounded by the enemy. He was a civilian now. He could let down his guard and the wall around his heart and allow himself to fall in love.

Was Abby the one? He'd only just met her. How could he be sure? Was love at first sight real?

The first time he'd seen Abby, she'd been covered from head to toe in mud, sticks and leaves. But even covered in all that dirt, he'd witnessed courage, strength and vitality in her. She was a fighter. Unsurprising, considering her occupation. No doubt handling a room full of fifth graders on a day-to-day basis was no easy feat. Oh, if those kids could have seen her the way he had the first time. He chuckled.

"What's so funny?" she asked as she reached the point where his shirt tucked into his jeans. Abby looked up into his eyes.

"I was just thinking about how you looked the first time we met," he admitted.

Her brow puckered. "I'm about to undress you

and that's what you think about?" She sighed. "Obviously, I need to up my game." Abby pulled his shirt free of his jeans, reached for the button at his waistband and flicked it through. She paused, pushed up on her arms and leaned over him. "If you don't want this, speak now," she said. "Because once I start, I'm not sure I can stop."

He grinned. "That should be my line."

Abby cocked an eyebrow. "You weren't forthcoming. Someone had to take the lead."

"I want this," he said, his voice deepening as desire flared, running like quicksilver through his veins.

A slow smile curved her lips as Abby bent over him and claimed his mouth with hers.

Her tongue thrust between his teeth and swept over his in a slow, sensuous glide.

Parker's hands curled around her hips and brought her over him.

Abby straddled him, the nightgown riding up her thighs, exposing every inch of her legs up to the edge of her panties.

Parker moaned. "Yeah, I want this." His fingers tightened around her hips.

Abby's lips left his mouth and traveled across his jaw and down the length of his throat. She flicked her tongue across his rapid pulse.

Not pausing long, she seared a path across his collarbone and his chest, stopping at one hard brown nipple. Her tongue flicked him there, causing a firestorm of sensations to spread throughout his body, culminating in his groin.

He tipped his head back and drew in a shaky breath. What she was doing was going to send him over the edge far too soon.

Parker inhaled deeply, tightened his hold on her hips and rolled her onto her back, coming up over her in a front-leaning rest position.

She blinked up at him. "Did I do something wrong?"

"No. Just the opposite. It was so right. I wasn't going to make it last more than a second or two. I want you. But I want you to want me, too."

Her lips spread in a sultry smile. "I already want you."

"Not like you will soon." He kissed her, tracing his tongue across her lips. When she opened to him, he teased her with gentle thrusts, touching her tongue and pulling back several times before taking more in a long, sexy caress.

From there, his mouth traveled down her neck, following the neckline of her nightgown to the deep shadows between her breasts. Balancing on one hand, he traced the fingers of his other hand up her torso and cupped the curve of one breast through the thin fabric of her gown. He pinched the nipple between his thumb and forefinger, rolling the tip as it tightened into a hard button.

Parker leaned down and claimed the nipple through the gown, sucking it into his mouth, flicking the tip with his tongue.

Abby's back arched off the mattress, a moan reverberating from deep in her throat.

Encouraged by her response, he abandoned the breast, gripped the hem of her nightgown and slowly drew it up, exposing more flesh, inch by inch.

She raised her hands over her head as he pulled the gown upward and off her body.

Abby lay against the mattress, wearing nothing but the thin scrap of material of her panties covering the tuft of hair over her sex.

Her breasts weren't overly large, but just enough to fill the palm of his hand.

He cupped both, squeezing gently. Then he lowered and took one into his mouth, gently pulling on the flesh.

Again, Abby's back arched off the mattress. Her hands moved from his shoulders to his head, her fingers weaving into his hair, urging him lower.

He obliged, liking that she wasn't afraid to let him know what she wanted.

Parker kissed his way down to the elastic waistband of Abby's panties and slipped his hand inside. The soft hairs curled around his fingers as he edged closer to her core. He dipped a digit into her slick channel. He wanted to take her then. Though she might be ready to accept him, she wasn't nearly close enough to her release.

Yet.

But she would be soon.

ABBY WAS ALREADY having difficulties breathing. Every time she drew in a breath, he touched her in a way that made her gasp.

Moving lower, Parker rolled to the side, took charge of her panties and stripped them down her legs, removing and tossing them across the room. He turned toward her, his gaze sweeping across every inch of her.

Abby lay naked against the comforter, turned on and hesitant at the same time. What if he didn't like what he saw? What if she wasn't experienced enough to satisfy him?

"You are beautiful," he said, his tone hot with his desire, melting into her bones like chocolate on a sweltering summer day.

"You're still wearing too many clothes," she said, her voice breathy, her lungs unable to pull in enough air to do any better.

He smiled, left the bed and stripped out of his jeans, kicking them to the side.

Her heart skittered through a quick succession of beats before settling into a racing rhythm.

Parker climbed onto the bed, slid his hands up the inside of her thighs and parted her legs, spreading them wide. He settled his body between them and kissed the sensitive skin from the bend in her knee all the way up her inner thigh to her core.

By then, Abby struggled to breathe. She felt like she teetered on the edge of a cliff, ready to soar to the heavens.

He parted her folds with his thumbs and touched her there with the tip of his tongue.

Abby gasped, drew her knees up and dug her heels into the mattress.

He flicked the nubbin of tightly packed nerves again and again.

Tension built inside her with every touch until she rocketed into the stratosphere, sensations exploding and spreading throughout her body.

She dug her fingers into his scalp and held on as wave after wave engulfed her, lifting her up, carrying her along until she slowly slid back to earth.

Adjectives like *great* and *good* didn't seem to encompass what she'd felt. All she knew was that it wasn't enough.

Abby tugged on his hair.

Parker crawled up her body, leaned over to fish his wallet out of his jeans and pulled out a small packet.

She grabbed it from his fingers, tore it open and rolled its contents over his engorged shaft.

He settled between her legs and bent to kiss her in a long, hard kiss that spoke of his intense concentration on controlling his own release.

Abby guided him to her entrance.

He dipped in slowly, coating himself with her juices.

Beyond patience, Abby gripped his buttocks and pulled him close, sheathing him in her channel.

Parker leaned his head back, his lips pressed

tightly together as he held still, giving her body time to adjust to his girth.

Again, Abby took control and eased him out and back in, working up speed until he took over and pumped in and out of her.

The tension built again inside her, matching the tightness of Parker's muscles and the control he clung to so precariously.

Abby quickly shot to her climax, lifting her hips to meet his thrusts with her own.

Parker slammed into her one more time, sinking deep, burying himself as far as he could go. He remained there, his shaft pulsing his release against her channel. His breathing was ragged as if he'd run a marathon and his body was coated in a fine layer of sweat.

Abby lay back, basking in the afterglow of making love with Parker, knowing she'd brought him to this level and he'd made sure she'd gotten there too. For a brief moment in time, she blocked the constant churn of all the awful scenarios the other captives might be facing and lived in the moment of making love with Parker.

"You should smile more often," Parker said as he eased down on top of her and rolled them both to the side, maintaining their intimate connection.

She draped her leg over his and laid her hand on his chest. "I will. When we free the others." She frowned. "I'm not usually so negative. I have to be upbeat to keep twenty-four students engaged every day."

He brushed a strand of her hair back behind her ear and brushed a kiss across her lips. "We'll find them. In the meantime, you need rest. You've been through a lot."

She rested her cheek against his chest, reassured by the strength of his muscles and the backing of his team. She wouldn't have to do this on her own. She had the Outriders behind her.

And he was right. She needed rest.

Tomorrow would come soon enough.

She prayed they'd find the house with the women alive and well inside.

But that would be too easy, wouldn't it?

Chapter Ten

Parker lay awake well after Abby drifted off. He couldn't believe how much she was coming to mean to him in such a short time. Frankly, it scared the hell out of him.

Not enough for him to get out of the bed and return to his room. No. He loved holding her close, feeling her warm, soft skin against his. He could get used to it. But he worried she would lose interest as soon as her world returned to normal.

He must have got to sleep shortly after midnight. When he glanced at the clock again, it was five in the morning and still dark outside with the barest of light in the predawn sky.

Abby lay on her stomach, an arm draped over his middle, her cheek resting on her pillow, blond hair hiding her face and eyes.

Parker lay still for a couple minutes memorizing every detail of the curve of her shoulder, the soft rose color of her lips and the scent of the shampoo she'd used.

Yeah. He could get used to waking up to this every day.

Today would be a challenge. One he needed to face sooner than later. He slid from beneath her arm, rose from the bed and dressed.

Abby rolled onto her side. Her hair slid away from her face revealing her closed eyes, the crescents of her lashes dark feathers against her cheeks. She was still asleep and Parker didn't have the heart to wake her yet.

He left the room and descended the stairs in search of coffee. The scent of bacon reached him before he arrived at the kitchen door.

Rosalyn stood at the stove, spatula in hand, turning over fluffy yellow scramble eggs in one skillet while bacon fried on a griddle.

"Coffee's made. All you need is a cup," she said.

"Thank you."

"I figure everyone will want to get out to the south fence before sunup and won't take time to eat, so I thought I'd make breakfast burritos for you to carry with you." She scooped the eggs out of the pan into a bowl and flipped the bacon over to cook on the other side. "I'll have them ready in just a few minutes."

"That's really nice of you. But you know you don't have to cook for us. We don't want to be more of a burden on your busy schedule."

She smiled. "I love cooking for people. I'm one of those people who need to be needed. It's my happy place."

Parker fished a mug out of the cabinet over the coffee maker and poured a cup. "Well, I appreciate everything you do."

"I just want to make it easier for you to get out there and find those girls."

He nodded and sipped the hot coffee, needing the caffeine boost to face the day.

"Irish and Matt got here a few minutes ago. They're outside now working with the drone, practicing with the controls and the livestreaming. I think they're getting the hang of it."

"Do you need help with the burritos?" Parker asked.

Rosalyn shook her head. "No, thank you. I have a system that works for me. I'll have them ready in no time. Lily and Trace are taking care of the animals. You might see if they need help to get done more quickly."

Parker took one more sip of the life-giving brew, set his coffee mug on the counter and stepped out onto the porch.

The whir of tiny rotor blades made him look up before descending the porch steps.

Matt and Irish stood next to Matt's truck. Irish had the laptop open on the truck's hood. Matt held the controls for the drone, maneuvering the two joysticks, a frown of concentration denting his forehead.

"How's it going?" Parker asked.

"Better," Matt responded. "I'm learning a little movement goes a long way."

"The camera on the drone is really sharp," Irish said. "Even in the semidarkness, it picks up more than I expected. And the livestreaming is working great. Let's hope it works as well away from the Wi-Fi."

"That's a good question. Will it work out there without immediate access to the internet?" Parker asked.

"I have a signal booster on my truck for my cell phone," Matt said. "It should allow us to access the internet through my hot spot."

Irish nodded. "We've tested it and it seems to work well."

"Unless you need me, I'm headed to the barn to see if Trace and Lily can use my help," Parker said.

"We've got it here," Irish said without looking up from the laptop display.

Parker continued past the two, glancing up to keep a watchful eye on the position of the drone as he crossed to the barn.

Inside, he found Lily and Trace pouring feed into buckets.

Lily looked up from the large feed bin. "We have the animals in the stalls. If you want to bring Jasper in, his stall is empty."

"He'll be all right for the day as long as he's grazing in the pasture." Parker glanced around. "Have you set out the hay?"

"Not yet," Trace said from where he was filling

a bucket full of water. "We usually put two sections in each stall."

Parker hurried to the stack of hay and broke open a bale. Pulling off several sections, he carried them to the stalls with horses in them and placed the hay in the wire hayracks attached to the walls. When he finished, he looked around. "What else?"

Lily, still scooping feed into buckets, nodded toward a large trash can. "That can contains the chicken feed. Take a coffee can full out to the coop and fill the feeder. You can collect the eggs in the empty coffee can. While you're out there, make sure they have fresh water."

Parker scooped a coffee can full of chicken feed and headed for the barn door.

"Hey, Parker," Trace called out. "Watch out for the rooster. He's a master at sneak attacks. I have the scars to prove it."

"I'll be on the lookout."

"There's a fishnet on the side of the chicken coop," Lily said. "If he gives you any trouble, scoop him up with the net and hang it on the outside of the chicken coop until you're done inside." She grinned. "I've never been spurred using that method. You can carry the can up to Rosalyn when you're done. We're headed that way soon."

Armed with chicken feed and knowledge, Parker carried the can out to the coop. As expected, the rooster stood guard at the gate, daring him to step inside. Parker grabbed the fishnet from a hook on the outside of the coop, opened the gate and scooped up the rooster. The beast protested loudly, but didn't have much of a choice about being hung on the side of the coop.

Parker poured the chicken food into the feeder and collected the eggs from beneath the nesting chickens, only getting pecked once in the process. He filled the water trough and released the rooster back into the coop.

The offended fowl shook out his feathers and went back to his position as guard in front of the gate.

By the time he returned to the house, Rosalyn had a dozen burritos rolled into plastic wrap and two thermoses full of coffee ready to go.

Abby stood next to Rosalyn, loading the food and drinks into a backpack, along with paper coffee cups and several bottles of water.

When she looked up and met Parker's eyes as he stepped through the kitchen door, her cheeks reddened.

"I'll take those." Rosalyn relieved him of the fresh farm eggs. "You're all set with food that should last you at least halfway through the day."

"The coffee won't make it halfway through the morning." Trace followed Parker through the back door. "But it'll do for a start." He smiled at his mother. "Thank you. You're a godsend."

Rosalyn gave a knowing smile. "I know." She glanced out the window. "You better get going before the sun comes up. You'll want to make use of every minute of daylight that you can."

"Yes, ma'am." Trace popped a salute. "You could have been a drill sergeant in another life."

His mother lifted her chin. "I could have been a drill sergeant in *this* life."

He dipped his head. "Yes, you could have. And a damned good one." Trace lifted his gaze to Lily. "Are you ready?"

"I am," she said, rubbing her wet hands on her jeans.

"After I wash my hands, I'll be ready," Parker said and headed for the bathroom.

Parker emerged from the bathroom to find Trace headed down the hallway, carrying an AR15 and a duffel bag and a sniper rifle slung on a strap over his shoulder.

"I have handguns and ammunition in the bag," he said. "Matt and Irish brought their own weapons."

"Is this all?" Parker asked.

Trace nodded.

"Let me carry some of that," Parker said.

Trace held over the AR15.

Parker took it and followed Trace out the back door to where the others had gathered around the truck.

Abby stood to the side with Brutus sitting quietly at her feet.

Trace laid out the plan as he loaded the weapons and bag into the back of his pickup. "We'll take two trucks. Parker, you and Abby will ride in my truck. Irish will ride with Matt."

Parker lowered the tailgate of Trace's pickup. "Brutus, up." The pit bull leaped into the back. "Stay."

"He won't jump out?" Abby asked.

"No." Parker scratched behind the dog's ear. "He learned how to be a ranch dog at the rehabilitation ranch."

Abby frowned. "Rehab ranch? I didn't know you'd spent time in rehab."

"How could you? We only met yesterday. We haven't had much time to get to know each other." A fact he meant to remedy soon. "Don't worry, it was for physical rehabilitation, not for drugs or alcohol." He opened the back door on the passenger side of the truck and handed Abby up into the truck. Then he rounded to the other side and slid in behind Trace, who sat in the driver's seat.

Matt stowed the drone and controls in the back seat of his truck and climbed into the driver's seat. Irish shut the laptop and climbed into the passenger seat.

Lily remained on the ground to open the gate. Once both trucks were through, she ran to climb into the lead vehicle with Trace.

They bumped along rutted tracks, across fields, down into streambeds and up over low hills.

Parker insisted on getting the next two gates, holding them open for the trailing truck.

Because Matt was familiar with the land and the direction they were headed, they covered the same amount of ground in less time than it had taken for Parker to ride Jasper to the same location.

Unlike the previous morning, the land and sky were clear of the dense fog.

The sun eased up on the horizon, a bright orange blob to the east.

"It's supposed to be a clear day with five to ten miles per hour winds," Trace said. "A perfect day for flying the drone."

Abby sat beside Parker, leaning around the back of Lily's seat to see their path ahead.

Parker spotted the uprooted tree and pointed. "See that dead tree? That's where we found Abby."

Trace brought the truck to a stop shot of the tree and the hollow where the roots had been and Abby had spent the night covered in dirt and leaves.

Parker recalled the shock he'd felt when she'd staggered to her feet like a creature born of the earth and ran from Brutus. When he realized it was a woman, he'd been even more shocked and afraid when Brutus attacked her, knocking her to the ground.

The dog had never attacked him or anyone else at the rehab ranch. Parker couldn't understand why he'd do it then. Until the shadow shapes of the feral hogs materialized through the fog.

"For the record," Parker said, "you were right... some of those hogs were as big as full-grown cows."

"Right?" Trace met Parker's gaze in the rearview

mirror. "The first time I saw one standing in the middle of the highway, I thought it was a cow." He shifted into Park and opened his door. "I wouldn't want to come face-to-face with one of those beasts."

"We came face-to-face with a herd of them yesterday." Parker cast a glance toward Abby. "Did you see them?"

Her eyes narrowed. "I think so, but it was hard to tell. Brutus had me pinned to the ground."

Lily opened Abby's door, her brow wrinkling. "Big ol' cuddly Brutus pinned you to the ground?"

"Big ol' terrifying pit bull with razor-sharp teeth, growling like he would rip my head off." Abby climbed down and reached into the back of the truck to scratch the monster's ear. "That's him. He didn't want me to run right into the middle of the hog herd."

Parker smiled at how quickly Abby had recovered from her fear of the pit bull and taken a shine to the big guy. He lowered the tailgate.

Brutus jumped to the ground and ran to where he'd found Abby.

Lily chuckled. "Do you think he's looking for another person to come out of the dirt?"

The dog sniffed the ground, ran a few steps and sniffed some more.

Parker crossed to see what the dog was so interested in. Hundreds of pig tracks speckled the ground around the hollow, and the dirt had been churned as if the hogs had been rooting in the soil.

Abby came to a stop beside Parker. "Are those pig tracks?"

Parker nodded. "Yes, ma'am."

She shivered.

"You might have chosen one of their favorite places to root around for grubs and bugs," Lily said.

Abby shivered again. "I might need another shower when we get back to the house. The thought of bugs and grubs crawling all over me gives me the willies."

"Better than hogs thinking you were part of their dinner," Lily said and turned to watch as Matt got out the drone and laid it on the ground, then reached for the control box.

Irish laid the laptop on the hood of Matt's truck and brought up the livestreaming video and the satellite map of the area, toggling between the two.

Abby and Lily gathered around the laptop while Trace and Parker converged on Matt.

Parker alternated looking at where the drone hovered several feet from the ground and glancing at the control box's monitor to understand what the camera would display.

"Ready?" Matt called out.

"Ready," Irish affirmed.

"Then let's get this party started." Matt lightly thumbed the tiny joysticks.

The drone rose into the air, heading south past where the fence was down and toward a line of hills dotted with live oak and juniper trees.

"What's the range of the drone?" Parker asked.

"It's a commercial drone with a range of almost five miles," Matt said.

"The challenge is that it has a battery life of only thirty minutes," Trace said.

"Five miles as the crow flies is a pretty good distance," Matt said.

"Running barefoot in the dark with a thunderstorm raging, rain hammering down on her head and over rough and hilly terrain, I doubt Abby got much further than that." Parker glanced back at Abby as she hovered over Irish's shoulder, her gaze intent on the images the drone was sending.

As it rose higher into the sky, the camera had a broader range.

Parker joined the women watching the larger monitor.

"If we can't make out much on this screen, we can spend more time looking at it on the large video screen in Trace's office back at the ranch," Irish said.

"The main idea is to get the video in the thirty minutes we'll have before the battery dies," Trace said.

"Make that an hour," Matt corrected. "I have one backup battery. And we can plug the charger into the truck and charge the dead battery while we use the backup. There might be some downtime, but not too much. I'm not sure how long it takes to fully charge a battery."

The first thirty minutes passed too quickly. Matt

chose landmarks to fly the drone between, establishing a kind of fan-shaped grid, covering a five-mile radius from the Whiskey Gulch Ranch property line.

They spotted a few straight lines that ended up being the tin roofs of deer stands, nothing as large as a two-story house.

By midmorning, Parker could see the disappointment and worry in Abby's face. He wished he could bear that burden for her. She looked tired.

Matt had grounded the drone while he waited for the battery to charge.

Irish had rewound the videos and was going over them, stopping every so often to zoom in on various areas that showed promise. With Lily, Abby and Trace looking over his shoulder, they didn't need Parker to add to the crowd.

His stomach rumbled, reminding him that none of them had eaten breakfast. He remembered the burritos Rosalyn had packed for them and went to Trace's truck in search of the bag she'd packed. He found it and the thermos of coffee, and returned to Matt's truck.

Parker handed a burrito and an empty paper cup to Matt who sat on the tailgate.

"I could skip the burrito, but the coffee is a must."

Parker unscrewed the thermos cap and poured coffee into Matt's cup. It was still hot and smelled good.

"Do I smell coffee?" Irish called from where he hovered over the laptop.

"Yes, you do," Parker said. He passed the thermos to Lily and distributed cups to Trace and Irish. When he tried to hand one to Abby, she held up her hand. "Not me. I never developed a taste for coffee."

"Good to know," Parker fished in the backpack for one of the bottles of water and handed it to Abby.

She smiled and took it. "Thank you."

Once everyone had drinks, Parker handed out the burritos.

"Eat them, even if you don't want one," Lily said. "Rosalyn went to a lot of trouble to make these for us."

"You don't have to tell me twice," Irish said. "Rosalyn makes the best breakfast burritos. She made enough for two each, right?"

"She did," Parker said.

By the time they finished their snack, one of the batteries had reached its full charge. Matt swapped out the batteries and put the dead one into the charger.

Becoming quite the expert, Matt had the drone in the air and headed down the next section of the grid.

Once again, Trace, Irish, Lily and Abby gathered around the laptop monitor.

Parker stood close to Matt, watching the smaller screen on the control box. The drone had reached the outer limit of its range and was headed back when a straight white line broke up the darker asymmetrical shapes of green, leafy live oak trees.

"Whoa," Parker said. "Can you get lower there?"

Matt brought the drone to a stop, hovering over a clump of trees.

"You see something?" Irish asked.

"Maybe." Parker leaned closer to Matt and pointed at the screen. "Can you back it up a bit?"

Matt eased the joystick and squinted down at the screen. "There?"

"Yeah. Hold steady." Parker turned and ran to where the others were studying the monitor.

"We have a slight delay in the livestreaming," Irish said.

Parker nodded. "You should see what we're seeing by now." He stepped between Lily and Abby and leaned over Irish's shoulder. It took him a moment before he found what he was looking for. "There." He pointed at the monitor. "See the white line?"

Irish leaned forward. "Yes."

"Matt, take it closer and swing around at a different angle," Trace said.

Matt eased the joysticks, sending the drone down and around the clump of trees. Approaching the trees from a different angle, the white line became the side of a white building. An old, two-story farmhouse.

Abby pointed with one hand and reached for Parker's with the other. "See that window under the A-frame roofline? Can you zoom in on it?"

Her fingers curled tightly around Parker's. He could feel her tremble.

Irish zoomed in on the window.

Abby gasped. "That has to be it."

"You said you broke the window. That window doesn't look broken," Trace said.

"They rehung the sheet over the window," Abby said. "If you notice, there isn't any glare or reflections of the sky or trees in the glass. Because there isn't any glass. And they removed the blanket I'd used to slow my slide over the roof."

"Matt, position the drone directly over the house," Trace said, "and save the coordinates. The rest of us will load up in my truck. We'll have to approach the house from the road. Matt, we need you here monitoring the location the best you can, given the battery life."

Matt nodded. "I have to bring in the drone now. The battery is getting low."

"Do it and get it back out there as soon as possible," Trace slipped into the driver's seat.

"I'm leaving Brutus with you." Parker turned to Brutus. "Come."

Brutus trotted over to where Parker stood near Matt.

Parker patted his head and then said, "Stay."

The dog maintained his position as Parker climbed into the back seat next to Abby. Lily slid in on the other side of Abby and Irish rode shotgun. Irish had the coordinates pulled up on the map on the laptop and the fastest route selected. Unfortunately, there weren't any roads nearby. They had to backtrack through the fields with Parker handling the gates. They wound up near the barnyard.

Rosalyn emerged from the barn.

Trace lowered his window and shouted as he sped past, "Found the house. Going to check it out."

"Be careful!" she shouted back.

Once Trace emerged onto the highway, he said, "Get Dallas on the phone. Tell her and Levi to meet us at the coordinates. If the house is occupied, we could use the help. If it's empty, we will want Dallas to get a crime scene unit out there."

Lily pulled out her cell phone. "Dallas, we think we found the house where Abby was held. I sent you the coordinates. We're on our way. Grab Levi and meet us there." She ended the call and slipped her phone into her pocket. "Should we have Dallas make this more official?" Lily asked.

"You mean bring in the sheriff's department?" Abby frowned. "That might take too long for them to get out there."

"We'll be there in ten minutes. It'll take Dallas and Levi at least fifteen. We'll stop half a mile short of the house and go in on foot. Lily, I'd prefer you and Abby stay in the truck until we give the all-clear."

Lily's mouth set in a tight line. "I can handle a gun."

Travis shot a quick smile in her direction. "I know how well you can. But Irish and Parker are trained Deltas. They know how to infiltrate a location, clear the rooms and when to shoot. Besides, I need you to stay with Abby and keep her safe in case the slime-balls comes up the road behind us."

Lily stared at the back of Trace's head for a long moment before she sighed. "Okay, I'll stay. I'd rather go with you, but I'll stay for Abby."

Trace smiled into the rearview mirror. "Thank you."

They turned onto a dirt road and drove for a couple of miles. Half a mile short of their destination, Trace pulled the truck off the road and parked it behind a fat juniper tree.

Trace leaped out, chose the sniper rifle and a handgun from the bag, and stuffed loaded magazines into his pockets. Parker grabbed the AR15 and a Glock 9 mm pistol and several magazines of ammunition.

It felt odd gearing up like he had prior to going into hostile enemy territory. But this wasn't Afghanistan, Iraq or any of the other foreign countries where they'd conducted special operations. This was the United States. A peaceful country. The land of the free and all that.

"You okay?" Trace asked.

Parker nodded. He shoved the magazines into his pocket and loaded one each into the rifle and the pistol. "I'm ready."

Lily selected a handgun from the bag, loaded it and stepped up to Trace. "Don't get yourself killed."

He pulled her close to him and kissed her hard. "I won't. I have too much to live for."

Abby touched Parker's arm. "You, too," she said softly. "Don't get yourself killed. I kind of like you."

"I like you, too." He cupped her cheek and bent to brush his lips across hers. "I'll be back for more of this."

Irish waited near the road with his own AR15.

Trace and Parker joined him.

"Consider this a reconnaissance mission," Trace said. "We'll observe first."

Irish and Parker nodded.

Together, they moved swiftly and silently, cutting through the woods.

Parker wasn't sure what they'd find. Hopefully, they'd find the women and their jailer, as Abby had called him. One guy would be easy to take down. Three or four? Still easy, just a little messier.

Chapter Eleven

Wearing the wig and sunglasses Lily had loaned her, Abby paced from the road to the truck and back to the road where she stopped, looked and listened, hoping to hear or see the team's progress.

Nothing.

They'd blended into the shadows and moved quickly, disappearing within the first twenty yards.

"They'll be okay." Lily stepped up beside her.

"I want to know what's happening," Abby said. "To see what they're seeing."

"I get it. I would like to have gone in with them." Lily held the gun at her side, aimed at the ground. "I do know how to handle a gun, but they're right. I don't have the training they do."

Abby wrapped her arms around her middle and rocked back on her heels. "Do you think they're up to the house yet?"

Lily laughed. "I really don't know. But we might want to step back from the road. If one of the men who kidnapped you comes along, we don't want to give him the opportunity to get you again."

"You have a gun," Abby said.

"That's right, but I'd rather not shoot someone unless I absolutely have to." She tipped her head toward the truck hidden behind the tree. "Want another one of Rosalyn's burritos?"

Abby shook her head. "I'm not hungry. But I imagine Laura, Rachel, Valentina and Cara Jo are." Abby followed Lily back to the truck. "I shouldn't have just left them."

"You didn't have time to pick the locks on their cages."

"No, but I should have stayed and fought."

Lily planted a hand on her hip and pursed her lips. "How big was he?"

"Pretty big. Maybe six feet three or four."

"Weighing around two-sixty or more?"

"Probably," Abby said. "Why?"

"Girl, unless you're highly skilled in self-defense, a man like that would easily overcome you and you'd be right back where you started from." Lily touched her arm. "You did the best thing you could do. And that was to get away as fast as possible. That way at least one of you could go for help."

Abby stared into the distance. "I hope the men find them alive."

"Me, too." Lily leaned against the truck and gave Abby a sly grin. "So, what exactly is going on between you and our newest Outrider?"

Heat climbed up Abby's neck into her cheeks. "Nothing." She continued to stare off into the distance, not willing to look Lily in the eye.

"That kiss wasn't nothing. I know it's none of my business, but Parker's bed wasn't slept in last night." She held up her hands. "I promise I wasn't snooping. I passed by his room early this morning and the door was open. And yeah, the bed hadn't been slept in." She shook her head. "Look, it's not any of my business who people sleep with. Lord knows, my family was notorious for what they did for a living. I'm just curious. You two just met, but you look at him like I look at Trace."

Her cheeks burning even hotter, Abby pressed her palms against them and glanced at Lily. "And how is that?"

A smile spread across Lily's face. "You look at him like you can't stand for him to be out of your sight. Like he hung the moon and stars and no one else exists in the world but him. That's how I feel about Trace. We had a rough start to our relationship, but now…he's my everything. I know I can live without him. I've done it before. But I'd rather live with him in my life and I'll do everything in my power to make him happy." Her smile broadened.

"And that's how I look at Parker?" Abby blinked. Not cool. "I barely know the man. Yeah, he saved my life, but that's not reason enough to fall in love with him in less than twenty-four hours." She frowned. "Is it?"

"I don't know about love at first sight. I can't re-member when I haven't loved Trace. I think I was born loving him." She shrugged. "I've heard women say, when you know, you know. One day, one month, one year? Everyone is different." She pushed away from the side of the truck. "I just hope you both don't get hurt. I know how bad it can hurt when the one you love doesn't love you in return." She paused, tilted her head to the side, her eyes narrowing. "Do you hear that?"

Abby lifted her head and strained to hear what Lily was hearing.

The rumble of an engine and the crunching sound of wheels on gravel increased in volume.

Abby peered around the juniper tree.

A plume of dust rose on the road.

"What do we do?" Abby asked.

Lily frowned. "We can't let anyone drive up to the house before the men are done."

"If it's more of the men who kidnapped us, we can't let them pass. And if we stop them, they might recognize me and blow our cover and put our guys in danger." Abby looked around. "Is there another gun in that bag?"

Lily nodded, reached into the bag, extracted a pistol and loaded a magazine full of bullets into the handle. "Do you know how to use one?"

Abby shook her head. "Not actually, but how dif-ficult can it be?"

Lily's eyes widened. "Oh, sweetheart. When we

get past all this drama, I'm going to teach you how to properly use a gun." She dropped the magazine from the handle of the gun, cleared the chamber and grabbed a baseball cap out of the bag instead. "Here, put this on and stay back. That vehicle is coming fast. I have to do something to slow it down."

Before Abby could stop her, Lily stuck the pistol in the back of her blue jeans and stepped into the middle of the gravel road and waved her arms.

Abby pulled the cap down low over her forehead, reached into the bag of hardware and retrieved the handgun Lily had put back and the magazine full of bullets. She inserted the magazine into the handle and eased up to the road, hiding behind the juniper tree.

"If they don't slow down," Abby called out. "Get out of the way."

"I will," Lily said. "I know you got that gun. Do me a favor and please don't shoot me."

Abby's hand shook. They'd have to be very desperate for her to fire the gun. It was strictly a last resort.

WHEN THEY WERE within a few yards of the house, Trace held up his fist.

Parker and Irish stopped immediately.

Trace motioned Irish forward. "While Parker and I check the house, you need to scout the perimeter for outbuildings, storm shelters or any other structure big enough for people to hide or be hidden in."

Irish nodded, backed into the woods and disappeared.

Parker moved forward and squatted in the shadows beside Trace.

Keeping low and in the shadows, Parker moved close to Trace.

"The place looks deserted," Trace whispered. "No vehicles and the front door is open. Lower windows are covered from the inside with cardboard."

Parker strained to hear anything from the interior. Nothing moved and no sounds came from inside. "I'll take point," Parker said.

Trace nodded. "I'll cover." He leaned against a tree, lifted his rifle to his shoulder and aimed it at the house. "Ready when you are. I'll leap in once you make the side of the house."

Parker nodded, glanced left then right and darted out of the trees, crossed the open space between the tree trunks and the walls of the building. Once there, he knelt.

Trace raced across the open space and into the shadow of the building. Once there, he didn't slow until he was up on the dilapidated front porch, moving quietly toward the open front door.

Parker followed.

Trace stopped short of the door.

Parker caught up to him, moved past and dove through the front door into the house. Tucking the rifle to his chest, he came up on his feet, aiming he AR15 toward the center of the room.

Not much light filtered through the overhanging branches of the giant old trees surrounding the house. Even in the dim light filtering through the door, Parker could tell the room was empty.

Trace ducked through the door and took position on the opposite side of the room.

Parker moved toward the back of the house. A hallway led past a staircase. With his foot, he pushed open the door to his right and aimed his rifle into a bathroom. Another empty room.

He continued down the hallway, emerging into a kitchen that probably hadn't been updated since the 1940s. It was empty. A couple of the cabinet doors hung off the hinges, revealing nothing inside.

Parker retraced his footsteps to the living room and covered Trace as he climbed a staircase to the second story. A door at the top of the staircase was closed with a shiny metal hasp hanging loose from the matching metal loop screwed to the door.

Trace dug a glove from his pocket, wrapped it around the door handle and turned it, pulling it toward him.

Parker lifted his rifle and covered Trace.

Trace disappeared into the room at the top of the stairs and reappeared. "Clear." He fished his cell phone out of his pocket and frowned. "Not much of a signal, but maybe enough." He tapped a text message and sent it. "I sent a text to Lily and let her know the house is empty. They can come up."

Moments later, a vehicle pulled up on the gravel drive and skidded to a stop.

Parker frowned. "That was fast."

Trace nodded. "Too fast." With his weapon in front of him, Trace eased up to the side of the window and peered out.

Parker moved up beside him.

"It's not my truck," Trace said.

Parker looked over Trace's shoulder.

The truck doors opened. Trousered legs dropped down below the driver's door. A handgun appeared first around the side of the open door. Dallas Jones stepped away from the truck and hurried toward the house.

Levi left the passenger side and followed Dallas across the yard.

Trace's shoulders relaxed and he chuckled as he moved toward the open front door. The truck was so filthy he hadn't recognized it. "Dallas, don't shoot, it's me, Trace Travis. I'm coming out."

He opened the door wider and stared into the barrel of Dallas's pistol.

"What part of don't shoot me, did you misunderstand?" Trace placed a finger on Dallas's gun and pushed it to the side, out of his face.

"When I didn't see you standing outside with no gun in your back, I wasn't going to risk it," she said and lowered her weapon.

Parker stepped up beside Trace. "We cleared the building. It's empty."

"I know. Lily told us you'd just texted her. You should have waited for us," Dallas said, lowering her weapon. "The place could just as easily have been occupied."

Levi stepped up beside Dallas. "Not here, huh?"

Trace shook his head and walked out onto the porch. "We were careful not to touch anything. Maybe you can lift prints."

Trace's truck pulled into the driveway and stopped next to Dallas's. Lily dropped down from the driver's seat. Abby got out of the passenger seat and approached the house, her eyes wide and haunted.

Parker dropped down off the porch and hurried to Abby. "I'm sorry."

She shook her head, tears slipping silently down her cheeks. "They're not here. I didn't get here fast enough."

"You can't beat yourself up about this," Trace said. "The place is clean. Most likely, they moved the others as soon as they discovered you'd escaped."

"I want to see," she said and climbed the steps to the porch.

Dallas caught her arm. "Don't touch any surfaces, especially door handles. The crime scene investigators will need to process the structure."

Abby nodded.

Parker took her hand and led her through the front door.

She stopped and stared at the empty room, a frown puckering her forehead. "There was a camp chair over there," she said, pointing to the right. "He had a battery-powered lantern next to it and empty pizza boxes."

Her gaze went to the staircase and the color drained from her face.

"You don't have to go any further," Parker said.

"Yes. I do." She started up the stairs, her feet moving slowly.

Parker followed behind her.

When she reached the top, she pressed her hand to her mouth and her shoulders shook with silent sobs. "We were here."

Parker slipped his arm around her waist and pulled her close. "We will find them."

"How? We don't know who has them or where they took them? They could be halfway across the country, or across the border in Mexico. I failed them."

He turned her toward him. "You didn't fail them. We're going to find them and get them home."

She stepped into his embrace and wept.

Parker's heart hurt for her. They had to find the women safe and sound and return them to their families.

Dallas and Lily entered the room and looked around.

Parker remained where he'd been standing. He held Abby until her sobs subsided into sniffles.

"Better?" he asked.

Abby nodded. "A little."

"Parker, Abby," Lily called out from the bottom of

the stairs. "We're heading back to the ranch to come up with a game plan for our next move."

"Coming," Parker responded without releasing his hold on Abby. He tipped her chin up and stared down into her red-rimmed eyes. "Ready?"

Abby stared back, her back stiffening. "I'm ready." She stepped back and squared her shoulders. "I'm not giving up. I owe it to them. Those women deserve to be saved, and I won't stop until I see that happen." She scrubbed her hand over her face, wiping away the tears. "I'm done crying. It's time for action."

Parker cupped her cheek and bushed away one of the tears she'd missed. "Let's do this." he took her hand and led her out of the house. Only Trace's truck remained in the driveway.

"We'll meet the others, including Matt and Brutus, back at the ranch," Trace said as he climbed into the truck.

"Will Dallas get any fingerprints?" Abby asked.

Lily shook her head. "The crime scene investigators will process the scene. They'll need your fingerprints to rule out yours." Lily slid into the front passenger seat and buckled her seat belt.

"I hope they find enough," Abby said.

Parker did, too. They didn't have much else to go on in their investigation.

He helped Abby up into the truck and closed her door. As he rounded the back of the vehicle, something white in the gravel caught his attention.

He bent and carefully brushed aside the dirt and lifted a piece of paper. He carried it with him as he climbed into his seat and buckled his seat belt.

"What's that?" Abby asked.

Parker shook his head. "I'm not sure."

"What did you find?" Trace asked.

Parker handed the crinkled, muddy document to Trace. "A temporary tag for a vehicle."

"Hold on to that," Trace said.

Parker nodded. "Dallas should be able to run the tag ID." He pulled out his cell phone and snapped a photo of the document.

"Send it to me. Lily can forward it to Dallas." Trace handed his cell phone to Lily.

Parker texted the photo to Trace's number.

Lily forwarded the text. "Dallas should have it now."

As Trace pulled out onto the gravel county road, he glanced in the rearview mirror at Parker. "I'll get you set up with a contact list of all the Outriders, their significant others and local law enforcement." He grimaced. "I need to set up a checklist for all new members."

"Yes, you do," Lily said. "Especially if you keep growing as fast as you have. I can be the administrative assistant, if you'd like."

Trace smirked. "In between running the ranch and keeping everybody and his brother fed?" He shook his head. "I'll hire someone else to manage the administration duties. You and Mom have enough on your plates. We still need to hire more ranch hands."

"Is there that much work?" Abby asked.

Trace nodded. "Yes, ma'am. And the more we do, the more word spreads and more jobs come our way. All by word of mouth."

Lily worked her cell phone, clicking keys and scrolling and clicking again. "There." She looked back at Parker. "I shared the phone numbers of the members of our team, Dallas, me and Rosalyn. You should be getting texts with those contacts."

Parker's phone dinged with each contact. He saved each of them to his list of contacts. "Thanks," he said.

Abby slipped her hand into Parker's and rode the rest of the way to the ranch, listening to Trace and Lily talk about different animals on the ranch and the operational issues.

When they arrived at the ranch house, Matt's and Dallas's trucks were there and empty.

Parker stepped down from the truck and was greeted by Brutus, whose entire body was wagging in pleasure at seeing Parker.

He patted the dog and scratched his ears as he rounded the truck to the passenger side.

Abby had already climbed down and stood beside the door.

Brutus transferred his attention from Parker to Abby, leaning his entire body against her knees in his happiness to see her.

Abby knelt to give the beast a belly rub.

"Traitor," Parker muttered. He pointed at Brutus. "Yeah. You."

Brutus licked Parker's finger and remained where he stood, leaning against Abby's legs.

Trace and Lily led them into the house, passed through the massive living room and turned down the hallway to his office.

Once through the office door, Parker could see the other members of his team perched on the leather sofa, leather chairs. Matt leaned his back against the stone fireplace at the other end of the room from Trace's desk.

"Good," Trace said as he strode into the room and slid to the side a large wooden wall panel, revealing a giant magnetic whiteboard. "For lack of a better term, I want to construct a timeline of the events leading up to Abby's escape."

Dallas fished several papers out of a satchel she'd brought into the house. "I have images of the victims you named, all subjects of missing persons reports, the dates they disappeared and the locations where they were taken."

Parker took the photographs and sorted them by date. He handed them to Trace one at a time.

Trace affixed them to the whiteboard in chronological order using magnetic clips.

Dallas pointed at the first girl's image. "Cara Jo Noble disappeared from Comfort, Texas, three weeks ago. Her parents reported her missing, believing she had possibly run away with her boyfriend who was also missing. When her boyfriend returned home without her, the local police opened an investigation. They questioned the teen who said she'd refused to come with him. That was eight days ago."

Abby nodded. "Cara Jo said she'd started home shortly after her boyfriend left her. She had just made it to the interstate to hitch a ride when she was picked up by a nice-looking young man, who appeared to be kind and friendly. She said he was blond with blue-gray eyes. Valentina indicated she'd been lured by a young man of a similar description."

Parker handed Trace the next photo. "Laura Owens disappeared a week ago."

"My contact said, she left her parents' home in Hondo on her way back to San Angelo where she attends college," Dallas said. "Her car was found at a truck stop on Interstate 10 where she'd apparently stopped to get gas. There was video footage taken at the gas station, but a big RV blocked the view of Laura pumping gas. She was there and then she wasn't."

"Can we get that footage?" Trace asked.

Dallas shrugged. "I don't know, but I'll see what I can do."

Parker handed Trace the next photo. "Rachel Pratt."

"Disappeared five days ago after she got a flat tire on Interstate 10 thirty miles from the Whiskey Gulch exit," Dallas said. "They found her car with her two small children. No sign of their mom. No witnesses. At the time, our department was notified to be on the lookout for her."

"Rachel said a young man stopped to help her. He wore a ball cap, so she didn't get a good look at his hair or eye color." She was just thankful for the help changing her tire. Until he threw her in the trunk of his car." Abby pressed a hand to her chest. "She was more worried about her children than herself."

"Valentina Ramirez," Parker handed the next photo to Trace, who affixed it to the board with a magnet.

"She's only sixteen." Trace shook his head.

"And so afraid," Abby drew in a deep breath. "She was walking home from the bus stop after school when a young man with blond hair and blue-gray eyes pulled up and asked for directions. Her mother must be beside herself. She said they were very close."

Parker put the last photo on the board, his chest tight as he pinned it with a magnet. "And the most recent abduction, Abby Gibson from Boerne, Texas."

Abby stared at the board, her face pale, her eyes shining with unshed tears. "They stole our lives."

Parker slipped an arm around Abby's waist. "And we're going to get them back."

"All the abductions were along the interstate between San Antonio and here, except Valentina." Dallas stood in front of the whiteboard, tapping her chin. "Hers was in one county over." She grabbed dry-erase marker and drew a line in a diagonal and wrote San Antonio at the bottom right and Whiskey Gulch at the top and added tick marks along the line where the women had been taken and added a box and marked their last known location, the house in the country.

Levi joined Dallas in front of the board. "I noticed a For Sale sign that had fallen over at the driveway entrance to the house where the women were held. It was a WG Realty sign. I think the listing agent was Celia Mann."

"Cecilia Mann," Matt corrected. "She's one of the agents at WG Realty. Nice enough woman in her fifties."

Dallas's cell phone rang. She glanced down at the number on the display. "I need to take this." She stepped out of the room into the hallway.

"We have to assume the people holding the women are from around here," Matt said. "How else would they know where to find an empty house?"

"Or know when a teenager gets off the bus and walks home alone," Lily said, her lips tight, her face grim. "That poor kid."

Trace continued to stare at the whiteboard. "We can ask the listing agent to see who is selling it and who has had access to it."

"And why the lock box was missing," Lily added.

Dallas returned to the room. "That was a contact of mine with the state police. I sent him an image of the fingerprints and the temporary tag."

Abby frowned.

Dallas held up her hand. "Since we think someone from around here might be involved and we didn't want locals to catch wind, I figured I'd work with an acquaintance in Austin."

"Good call," Trace said.

Abby nodded.

"Anyway, only one of the prints struck pay dirt." Dallas glanced at her phone. "A Roy Felton, convicted felon, registered in this county. I have his address. He was convicted of aggravated assault, spent two and a half years in prison, and was paroled a couple of months ago. He works at Greenway Lawn Care in Whiskey Gulch."

"We'll check it out," Trace said. "What about the tag?"

"Belongs to a car registered to one Scott Wilcox, also from Whiskey Gulch," Dallas said. "He's clean. No criminal record. I have his address."

Trace clapped his hands. "The workday isn't over yet. We can hit a few of these places and ask some questions. Matt and I will check out Roy's home address. Levi and Dallas, see if you can meet with Roy's parole officer."

"Just so you know," Dallas said. "I work graveyard tonight. After we check in on Roy, I'm headed to the house for a few hours' sleep before I'm on duty."

"Noted," Trace said. "Irish and Becker, check in with the Scott." He turned to Parker.

"We'll go to the real estate company and find out who owns the house," Parker said.

"We?" Trace cocked an eyebrow, his gaze going to Abby. "Are you sure you want to be seen in Whiskey Gulch?"

Lily stepped in. "I'll get another wig and sunglasses." She left the office, passing Rosalyn in the doorway.

"Sorry to interrupt," Rosalyn called out. "I need to know how many will be having dinner here."

"We'll grab something in town. You don't need to be cooking after working with the farrier all day."

She pushed a stray strand of hair back from her forehead and gave him a tired smile. "Good. I think I'll go soak in a hot bath and call it a night." She turned to leave, calling out over her shoulder, "If you don't feel like eating in town, you can make sandwiches when you get back. There's plenty of cold cuts and cheese in the fridge."

When she was gone, Trace said to the people in the room, "Don't forget to grab dinner while you're in town. Everyone know their assignments?"

Parker nodded along with the others.

"Let's go," Trace said.

Lily appeared with the wig and glasses.

Abby thanked her and carried the items out to Parker's truck.

"Are you sure about this?" he asked as he helped her up into the passenger seat.

She met his gaze with a stubborn tilt of her chin.

"Absolutely. I promised to bring help. And, dammit, I will."

Parker hurried around and climbed into the driver's seat. He hoped the information they had would lead them to the women. Seeing their photos on the board along with Abby's had brought it closer to home. They weren't just names. Those women were mothers, daughters, wives and granddaughters to someone. If he had a daughter, how would he feel if she was kidnapped and sold into the sex trade? He glanced at the woman beside him. How would he feel if his wife were kidnapped and sold?

He drove off the ranch. Once he hit the highway, he pressed hard on the accelerator. The sooner they found the women, the better.

More than that, they had to find everyone involved and put them out of commission.

Chapter Twelve

While Parker looked up the address of WG Realty, Abby pulled back her hair, secured it in a tight bun and slipped the black wig over her head. She tucked in the stray blond hairs and viewed herself in the mirror on the visor.

"It's not me, but that's the point." She added the sunglasses and applied the lipstick Lily had provided.

Parker grinned. "A complete transformation. No one will recognize you."

She sat staring at the road ahead, her thoughts miles ahead, composing what she would say to the real estate agent. "I think we should approach the agent as if we were a couple looking for a private retreat. The further off the beaten path the better."

"Agreed. This agent might not know what was happening in that house. We don't want her to inadvertently alert anyone who might be involved."

Abby nodded. "We could say we were driving around and found their sign and were interested in the property. We could ask how long it had been on the market and if she could share anything about the history of the old place and the people who lived there."

"She could also point us in the direction of other remote properties that are currently vacant," Parker said.

"Places they might have moved the women to." Abby nodded.

Parker pulled into a small parking lot in front of a building on Main Street in Whiskey Gulch. A sign over the door read WG Realty.

Abby's pulse kicked up.

A strong hand reached across the console and gripped hers. "Are you okay?"

"I've never worked an undercover operation." She laughed. "Fifth grade teachers aren't usually called on for that kind of work."

"You'll be fine," he said. "You look amazing, like a cover model incognito. The agent will think you're a celebrity or something."

"And I married my bodyguard?" She smiled. "Ha. And I'm completely opposite. Oh, and did I tell you? I'm a terrible actress in front of adults." She gave him a tight smile. "Let's get this over with."

Parker chuckled as he got down from the truck and round the hood to the other side. He helped her to the ground and offered her his elbow.

She linked her arm through his and smiled up at him like a lover. And weren't they just that? Especially after the previous night's mattress gymnastics.

He'd been a gentle and considerate lover, concerned about her needs and satisfaction. What more could a woman ask for?

He held the door for her and followed her in.

A receptionist looked up from her computer screen. "Can I help you?" she asked.

"We'd like to speak with Cecilia Mann," Parker said.

The woman smiled. "Let me see if Ms. Mann is available. What name shall I give her?

"Shaw," Parker said. "Mr. and Mrs. Shaw."

A twinge of joy rippled through her. She liked the sound of that. Maybe a little too much for having just met the man.

She lifted a desk phone receiver and tapped a button. "Ms. Mann, Mr. and Mrs. Shaw would like to meet with you. Are you available?"

The woman listened and nodded. "I will. Thank you." She set the receiver back in its cradle and smiled up at Parker and Abby. "She'll be with you in a moment." She stood and waved a hand toward a glassed-in room. "If you'll follow me, you can have a seat in the conference room." She led the way into the room. "Can I get you something to drink? Coffee, water, a soda?"

"I'd like water," Abby said. Anything to keep her hands busy and prevent fidgeting.

Parker held up his hand. "Nothing for me, thank you."

The receptionist disappeared and returned with a chilled bottle of water, handed it to Abby and left.

Abby twisted off the top and drank half the bottle, thirstier than she'd thought. After three days in captivity with little food or water, she could use it.

A woman with a stock of white hair entered the room with a smile. "My apologies for keeping you waiting. I was on the phone with a client who will be closing on her new house tomorrow." She sat at the end of the table where a laptop lay closed neatly on the surface. She folded her hands in front of her and gave them her complete attention. "What can I help you with? Looking for a house, land or a builder?"

Abby glanced over at Parker.

He smiled at the woman. "Parker Shaw and this is my wife, Amy."

"Cecilia Mann," she said and shook Parker's hand and then Abby's. "Nice to meet you both."

"We're new to the area and interested in a country setting with acreage and privacy." He smiled at Abby. "My wife is a writer. She needs to limit distractions to allow her to focus on her work."

"Really?" Cecilia raised her eyebrows and directed a glance in Abby's direction. "Amy Shaw... I love to read. I wonder if I've read any of your books."

Writer? Abby fought to keep from glaring at Parker for making up the lie that she now had to propagate. She forced a tight smile. "I doubt it. There are so many books available to read. We've been driving around the county just trying to get the lay of the land and areas we'd be interested in living. We found you because there was a particular home on a gravel road in the middle of nowhere that could be perfect with some remodeling."

"Well, let me look it up," she said and opened the laptop. After it booted, she clicked on the keyboard and paused. "Address?"

Parker shrugged. "We're not quite sure. It's quite secluded and we didn't see a street number." He gave her the name of the road.

"I should be able to find it," Cecilia said with the confidence of a seasoned Realtor. She entered the road name and waited for the system to bring up a map of the properties in that area. She reached for a remote control in the middle of the table and clicked a button on it. A large monitor flickered to life on the far wall with a map of the road and the properties on either side.

"I don't see any actually for sale." She frowned. "I seem to recall listing a house on that road at one time. I don't think it actually sold. It needed too much work, if I remember correctly. I might have forgotten to pick up the sign."

"Oh, we don't mind a fixer-upper," Abby said. "And we love older homes with a history."

Cecilia clicked on a property and a picture of the house flashed up on the screen. "Is this the house you saw?"

"Yes," Abby said, her heart pounding wildly in her chest.

"I remember this one. The owners were an elderly couple unable to live on their own anymore. They moved in with their daughter in Houston. They tried to sell the house, but their daughter and her husband just didn't want to deal with it. They think the house should be bulldozed to the ground and the land sold. But they don't want to upset her parents while they're still alive. So they left it to me to list it for as long as it takes to sell it."

She waved a hand at the screen on the wall. "Would you like to look at it?"

"We'd like for you to put together several options for us to drive by before we ask to see the insides," Parker said. "We're looking for two to ten acres of land and enough room for our dogs to run where they won't disturb neighbors. The more remote the better. And since we're having to stay in a hotel right now, vacant homes would be best. The sooner we get moved in, the better."

Cecilia frowned at the laptop. "That's odd," she said. "The house you're inquiring about shows that it's been delisted." Her brow furrowed. That was my listing. I don't remember the owners calling to have me pull the listing."

"Can anyone remove a listing?" Abby asked.

"Usually, the agent who listed it is the only one who can remove it," she said. "Or someone else within her agency. I'll check into it and pull some other potential homes meeting your criteria and send you the links if you'll leave your phone number or email address." She slid a pad of paper and pen toward him.

Parker scribbled his cell phone number on a pad. "When can we expect to hear from you?"

"Oh, I'll get right on it," she said. "I'll have some options to you within the hour. Look over them and call me with the ones you'd like to tour."

Parker pushed to his feet and held Abby's chair as she rose. "Thank you for your time, Ms. Mann. We look forward to hearing from you."

The Realtor beamed. "Thank you for choosing WG Realty for your housing needs."

As they rose to leave the conference room, a barrel-chested, silver fox of a man appeared in the doorway with a smile. "Good afternoon," he said, his voice booming in the confines of the office. He held out a hand to Parker. "Brandon Marshall."

Cecilia smiled. "Brandon, this is Parker and Amy Shaw. They're new to town and looking for a home. Parker, Amy, Brandon is the owner of WG Realty."

Parker gripped the man's hand and shook.

Brandon winced and pulled his hand free quickly.

He reached for Abby's hand next, his eyes narrowing for a split second as he studied her face. The man's smile never slipped. "Nice to meet you two. Is Cecilia helping you out?"

"Yes, she is," Parker said.

"They're interested in the old Golenski place," Cecilia nodded toward the image on the big screen.

"I told them it needs a lot of work, but that it's vacant and they're eager to get settled."

Brandon's eyes narrowed again. "Is it even on the market?"

"That's what's strange." Cecilia's brow wrinkled. "I listed it. When our contract expired, I called them. The owners said to leave it up. When I went online a minute ago to look at the listing, it showed as inactive. If this nice couple hadn't seen our sign out there, I might never have known it wasn't showing on the system." She smiled at Parker and Abby. "It's so good that you came in today."

"When did you go out there?" Brandon asked.

"Just a little while ago," Parker said.

"It's a lovely, peaceful location," Abby said. "We liked the big trees and the seclusion."

"It's definitely secluded," Brandon said in his big voice.

"I'm going to pull a few listings to show them tomorrow or the day after," Cecilia said.

"If you'll excuse us," Parker laid a hand on the small of Abby's back and urged her forward. "We didn't have lunch today and would like to find somewhere to have an early dinner."

"Try the diner," Cecilia said. "Their food is good no matter what time of day."

"Nice to meet you, Mr. Marshall," Abby said.

Parker steered her past the reception desk and out into the parking lot.

Neither spoke until they were inside the truck

with the windows rolled up and they were driving out of the parking lot.

"Convenient that the listing had been delisted, don't you think?" Parker said.

"Like Cecilia said…odd. The whole visit was odd." Abby couldn't quite describe the level of unease she'd felt the entire time she'd been in the realty office.

"What do you mean odd?"

"I can't put my finger on it. Maybe it was the house that leaves me with bad vibes. Or the fact that the listing had been delisted, especially for the time when five women were being held hostage in the attic." She shrugged, trying to dispel that oppressive sense of doom.

Parker shot a glance in her direction. "Think Cecilia is in on this operation?"

"No," Abby said. "But it wouldn't hurt to have Dallas run a background check on the agents who work at WG, including Brandon Marshall."

Parker handed her his cell phone. "Would you do the honors and send that text to Dallas?"

Abby took the phone, keyed the message and sent it to Dallas. "Didn't she say she works the graveyard shift again tonight?"

Parker nodded. "She did."

"Then she might have time to do some computer sleuthing if she's not out on patrol the whole night."

"We should also see if Trace has some internet contacts who can dig deeper." Parker pulled into a parking space in front of the diner, shifted into Park and turned off the truck. "Hopefully, the other guys have had more luck with their assignments."

Abby nodded. She worried they wouldn't find the women in time.

As they entered the diner, a petite waitress with silky brown hair and bright green eyes sailed by them with a smile. "Find a seat. I'll be back with a menu."

Parker steered Abby to a corner booth and sat with his back to the wall.

Abby smiled. "Do you always sit with your back to the wall?"

He nodded. "Doesn't hurt to be where you can see what's coming and going. Situational awareness at all times."

She scooted out of her seat and stood. "Move over," she said.

Instead of scooting, Parker stood.

"Don't tell me you also like to be on the outside, too." She shook her head and slid into the booth all the way over.

Parker sat beside her.

The waitress handed them laminated menus. "I'm Misty. I'll be your server. What would you like to drink?"

"Water for me," Abby said.

"Water and a cup of coffee," Parker said.

Misty disappeared and returned quickly with a tray holding two glasses of water and a cup of coffee. "Do you need more time to order? I'd go for the country fried steak. Joe makes the best. It's the special for the day."

"Sounds good," Abby said, liking the perky young woman. "I'll have that."

"Me, too," Parker said.

Misty took their order to the kitchen and was out in the dining room seconds later, filling glasses and fetching items for other customers.

A man in a sheriff deputy's uniform stepped through the door and looked around, his gaze going to the table where Parker and Abby sat. His eyes narrowed briefly.

"Sonny!" Misty the waitress called out as she emerged from the kitchen. She hurried forward, wrapped her arms around his waist and kissed him. "What a nice surprise. Are you staying?"

"Can't," he said. "I'm on duty. Thought I'd stop and see my best girl."

She smiled. "Thanks. Nice to know the county's finest is around to protect the blue-collar residents of Whiskey Gulch." She danced away. "Don't forget we have a date this weekend."

"About that..." he started.

"Not again," Misty pouted.

Parker leaned toward Abby. "You're eavesdropping, aren't you?" he asked.

"Totally," Abby said. "They're such a cute couple. It's hard to look away. And when he smiles, I can see why Misty is so into him. He's gorgeous."

"Whoa. Wait. You're *my* wife," Parker said with a crooked grin. "Don't go making me jealous."

"Shh." Abby touched a finger to her lips. "I can't eavesdrop if you're talking at the same time."

"Yes, ma'am," he said.

The deputy had Misty in his arms again. "Sorry, babe. I'm flying down to Mexico." He ran his hand through his blond hair, making it stand on end. "You know my friend I've told you about? Well, he had a motorcycle wreck and is in the hospital. I'm leaving as soon as I get off, and won't be back until Sunday."

Misty touched his arm, a frown denting her brow. "I'm sorry to hear that. And I'm sorry you won't be here. I bought the cutest black skirt with long black fringe." She sighed and moved her hand on his chest. "I was going to wear it the first time just for you."

"I'll take a rain check on that skirt."

"You know…" Misty walked her finger up his chest. "You wouldn't have to take a rain check if you took me with you to Mexico." She looked up at him and batted her eyelashes. "I have my passport and I've never used it."

"I don't know…" he said. "I have a friend flying me down. I'd have to see if he can take another passenger."

Her face lit up. "Then ask him. I'm off in fifteen minutes. You can pick me up, take me by my place. I can pack in no time. Please say yes."

He stared at her a moment longer and finally nodded. "I'll ask. Are you sure you'll be done in fifteen minutes?"

She nodded, already untying the apron around her waist.

"Okay, then. I'll clear it with the pilot and be back." The young deputy kissed her again and flashed his engaging smile.

Abby blinked at how charismatic the man was and how his blond good looks complimented Misty's dark hair and green eyes. How fun would it be to fly off at a moment's notice to Mexico with the man you loved?

The deputy left the diner, slid into his service vehicle and drove away.

Misty snagged the coffeepot and hurried to their table, her cheeks pink. "Sorry for the delay. My boyfriend doesn't always understand that I have to work. Now, what can I get for you?"

"Your boyfriend works for the sheriff's department?" Abby asked.

The young woman's head bobbed. "What can I say, I love a man in uniform. And he always brings me presents when he comes back from Mexico." She reached up and tapped one of her earrings. "He gave me these a couple of days ago." She leaned close to Abby. "Aren't they beautiful?"

Abby nodded. "Yes, they are."

Half-moons made of silver and mother-of-pearl dangled from Misty's earlobes. "Don't you just love them?"

"I do." Abby smiled.

The waitress topped off Parker's coffee. "I'll be back with your food. Then I'm headed out. Margie will cover your table after I'm gone."

The diner door opened again. Trace and Matt entered and looked around.

Parker raised one hand.

The two men joined Parker and Abby, sitting in the booth across from them. "Anything?" Trace asked.

Parker shook his head. "Not much. Only that the house was on the market and then it wasn't. Cecilia Mann is the listing agent, but she doesn't remember delisting it. The owners are elderly and moved closer to their kids. They're not in a big hurry to sell."

"I feel like there's more to the story." Trace said.

"Obviously, but I don't think the owners are involved." Abby frowned. "Someone knew the house was empty and decided to squat."

"What did you find at Roy's place?" Parker asked.

Trace's lips pinched together. "He wasn't there. His snoopy cat-lady neighbor said he hadn't been there for several days." Trace's cell phone rang. "That'll be Irish and Becker." Trace pushed to his feet and walked out of the diner.

"When the waitress comes around, we need to order coffee for two," Matt said.

Misty returned with Trace and Abby's food and set it on the table in front of them. She took Matt's drink and food order, stopped to talk to another waitress and headed for the kitchen.

Trace returned to the table and slid in next to Matt. "That was Dallas. She and Levi visited Roy's parole officer. The man said Roy was doing good until about a couple weeks ago and then he stopped checking in. If Roy doesn't check in soon, the officer will have him arrested. He said Roy worked for Greenway Lawn Care as a day laborer. They spoke to the manager there and found that Roy hadn't shown up for work for over a week."

"Did they have a description of Roy?" Abby asked.

"Yes. They said he was hard to miss, standing at six feet four inches."

"Sounds like our jailer." Abby hugged herself around the middle, remembering how strong Roy was and how she'd been helpless to break free of his grip.

Trace continued. "Irish and Becker went to check on the owner of the car with the temporary tag."

"Did they find the car?"

Trace nodded. "It was clean. I mean clean. Not a single fingerprint on it. Someone wiped it down. Irish got under the chassis and found the dirt. Literally. The SUV had been on a dirt road. When they'd washed it, they hadn't taken into account the amount of mud caked to the undercarriage."

"So? There are a lot of dirt roads in the county," Parker said.

"But this vehicle was on that particular dirt road the night of the storm, and whoever was driving it, went to the trouble of cleaning it and wiping away the fingerprints," Matt said.

"So, is Scott Wilcox involved?" Abby asked.

Trace shook his head. "No. Irish called him. He's been in New Jersey for three months. He'd ordered the SUV to be delivered to his house. His plan was to come and get the new vehicle this weekend from his house."

"You say Scott had the car delivered," Parker said. "Where did he purchase it?"

"At a local dealership, managed by William Dutton," Trace said. "They stopped by the car lot, but William Dutton wasn't there. I remember Will Dutton from high school."

"I do, too," Matt said, his eyes narrowing. "Wasn't he a defensive lineman on the football team a couple years ahead of us?"

Trace nodded. "A big guy."

"A bully," Matt added, his lips pressing together. "He liked to push people around on and off the field."

Trace nodded. "He must have straightened up after high school to land a job managing a car dealership."

Parker's phone dinged with an incoming text. He glanced down at the message on the screen. "Cecilia just sent some potential homes for the *wife* and I to look over." He winked at Abby and pulled up the first link on his cell phone.

"How many did she send?" Trace asked.

Parker counted the list. "Ten."

"Good grief. That would take some time to check all of them," Matt said.

"And those are the active ones," Parker pointed out. "They'd delisted the first house before moving in to make sure no one came out to show it to a potential buyer. It would be too risky to stash the women in an active listing."

Trace's phone buzzed with an incoming text. He read the message and frowned. "This from Dallas. She stopped by the sheriff's office and did some asking around about Brandon Marshall. She talked to his former girlfriend. Apparently, he's in debt up to his neck and has defaulted on a couple loans, including the loan on his personal airplane."

Parker leaned over the table to look at Trace's phone. "Did Dallas share Marshall's tail number for his plane?"

"Let me look," Trace stared down at his phone. She sent some of the documents filed with the state." He scrolled through the text and stopped. "Here."

Parker brought up an app on his cell phone and keyed in the tail number. "This app tracks the flight plans of airplanes by their tail numbers or flight numbers. That plane has made a number of flights to Mexico in the past few months."

Mexico.

Abby's gaze followed Misty as she poured coffee, settled checks and greeted each customer with a friendly smile.

Mexico.

Something wasn't sitting right with her. She felt like she was finding pieces to the puzzle, but she hadn't figured out how to fit them together yet. She wanted to talk with Misty about her boyfriend and their proposed trip to Mexico.

Misty was waving to her coworkers and heading for the back of the restaurant.

"Why would a real estate agent whose business is in Texas go to Mexico so many times?"

"Maybe he has a vacation home there," Matt said. "Lots of Texans do."

Parker held up his phone with a picture of an airplane. "This is the model aircraft he owns. It's not just a little recreational plane. It's a turbo prop that can take eight to ten passengers and their luggage."

"No wonder he can't make the payments on it. Those cost in the millions," Trace said.

Abby's heart beat faster as the puzzle pieces started sliding into place. "What if—"

Before she could voice her thoughts, a horn blared, tires squealed and an older model tank of a car crashed into a jacked-up, four-wheel-drive pickup in the diner parking lot.

Parker, Matt and Trace leaped from their seats and ran out the door. Abby followed, stopping short of the threshold. A dozen people gathered around the car where a little, old woman sat behind the wheel, stunned and shaken.

With all the people out front helping, they didn't need Abby. But someone else might.

She turned and walked through the swinging kitchen door.

The woman Misty had called Margie stood near a large vat of hot oil. She lifted a basket of fries out of the oil and dumped them into a bin.

"Margie?" Abby called out.

"That's me," she looked up from sprinkling salt over the hot fries.

"Which way did Misty go?" Abby asked.

Margie tipped her head toward the rear exit. "Her shift was over. She left through the door back there. Do you need me tell her something?"

"No, thank you. I can do that."

Margie snorted. "If you catch her."

Abby sprinted for the door. Hoping she wasn't too late.

Misty was about to go to Mexico with the deputy, someone people would trust because of his friendly face, easy smile and his uniform.

Abby walked faster and broke into a run down the hallway to the exit door.

Brandon Marshall owned a plane and a real estate agency. He had knowledge of and access to vacant properties. He went to Mexico often in a plane that could hold eight to ten people.

Maybe she was adding two and two and coming

up with seven, but she felt compelled to warn Misty not to go to Mexico.

She burst through the back exit as Sonny climbed out of an expensive-looking black car and smiled at Misty.

"Misty," she called out.

The waitress turned back, a frown pulling her eyebrows down. "I'm sorry," she said. "Did I forget something?"

Abby couldn't think fast enough to come up with anything other than, "Don't go."

"Excuse me?" Misty's frown deepened.

Abby's gaze met Sonny's. "Don't go with him to Mexico," she said in as calm a voice as she could muster.

"Why?" Misty asked.

Behind Misty, Sonny's brows descended into a dangerous glare. "Yeah. Why?"

"It's…dangerous," she said. Now that she'd barged into their escape, she wondered if she'd read too much into the deputy's handsome face. If he wasn't the man who'd lured Cara Jo and Valentina into his vehicle, Abby would be embarrassed.

If he was one and the same, she could possibly have thwarted his attempt to kidnap Misty and sell her in Mexico with the other four women.

His lip curled back in a sneer. "Your hair is crooked," he said, pointing to her wig.

When she reached up to straighten the wig, she realized her mistake.

Sonny reached behind his back and pulled out a handgun, wrapped his arm around Misty and pointed the gun to her temple.

"Sonny, what are you doing?" Misty cried.

"Shut up," he said. His gaze on Abby, he waved the gun toward the rear of the car. "Get in the trunk."

She backed a step, shaking her head. "No way." Having been a prisoner before, she'd rather die than be one again.

"Get in the trunk or I hurt her." He pressed the tip of the barrel to Misty's temple.

"Sonny, you're scaring me," Misty whimpered.

Abby's gut clenched. "Let her go, Sonny. If you fire a shot, everyone will hear it and come running."

"What are you doing?" Misty whispered. "I thought you liked me."

"I'm taking care of business," he said. "You," he tipped his chin toward Abby. "Get in the trunk. Now." He looped his arm around Misty's throat and tightened his hold.

Misty's eyes widened and her hands rose to claw at the arm around her neck. "Sonny," she said, her voice barely a whisper. "Don't."

His gaze held Abby's. "Get in the trunk, or her death is on you."

In the back of her mind, Abby knew better. Misty's death was all on Sonny. But the fear and desperation in Misty's eyes tore at Abby's heart. "Let her go and I will," she said.

"Get in first, and I'll let her go." Still, he held her gaze, his arm unrelenting in its hold on Misty.

The woman's struggles weakened. If Abby didn't do as he said soon, she'd be dead.

Abby walked slowly toward the car, praying Parker would notice she was gone before she made it into the trunk.

"Move," the deputy ground out.

Misty's hands slipped from his arms and fell to her sides.

Abby stood at the trunk, dread filling her soul. Sonny stepped up behind her, slammed the butt of his pistol against her temple and shoved her hard.

Abby fell into the back of the car, her head spinning, darkness closing in around her. She fought the darkness, knowing she had to stay awake and alert to find another way out of this mess.

Something heavy landed on top of her and dark brown hair fell into her face.

He'd dumped Misty's limp body in the trunk with her and closed the lid.

Chapter Thirteen

When the vehicles crashed in the parking lot in front
of the diner, Parker, Trace and Matt had reacted immediately, rushing out to help.

The old woman in a vintage Cadillac sat shaking behind her steering wheel, tears pouring down
her cheeks. Parker tried to open her door, but it was
jammed shut. When Matt yanked open the back door,
a small ball of white fluff leaped out and ran.

"Sweetpea!" The old woman screamed, "Catch
her! Don't let my baby get away."

Matt dove after the little dog.

It ran in the opposite direction.

Trace grabbed for her.

The little white rat of a pup evaded him as well.

Park stepped in front of it. "Sweetpea, stay," he
commanded.

She dashed between his legs.

"Abby, grab her!" he yelled and spun.

Abby wasn't behind him. The white fluff ball ran

under a parked car and stopped, hiding behind one of the tires.

Parker looked back at the woman in the old car.

She waved at him. "Don't worry about me, I'm not going anywhere. Catch my Sweetpea."

He dropped to the ground next to the car, reached around the tire and snagged the dog by its long hair.

She wiggled but couldn't get loose.

He rolled to his feet holding the frightened dog in his arms.

Sweetpea shook, she was so traumatized.

"Oh, thank God," the woman said and cried grateful tears.

A siren wailed in the distance as a fire truck and an ambulance raced toward them, lights flashing.

Parker handed Sweetpea to a female bystander. "Hold her. Don't let her go. Her name is Sweetpea."

The woman nodded. "I've got her."

Parker joined Matt and Trace as they stood back, watching the fire fighters pry open the Cadillac.

"Have you seen Abby?" Parker asked.

Trace looked around him. "I thought she was with you."

"No," Parker said. "I haven't seen her since we left the diner. I'll go see if she's there." He hurried toward the front door of the diner looking all around him as he did. All the while, a sense of impending doom filled his chest.

"Abby!" he called out. "Abby!"

Parker pushed through the door, his gaze shooting to the booth he'd shared with her.

It was empty and clean, as if they'd never sat side by side on the bench.

"Abby," he called out softly. Then louder. "Abby!" He ran down the short hallway to the ladies' room, pushed the door open slightly and called out her name again.

No one answered. He went in and checked the stalls. Empty. No Abby. Hurrying back out into the dining room, he yelled, "Abby!"

"Can I help you?" the waitress named Margie emerged from the kitchen, carrying a tray loaded with plates full of food.

"I'm looking for the woman who came in with me. She has blond-black hair."

Margie nodded. "She went out the back through the kitchen, trying to catch Misty before she left with Deputy Tackett. That was a few minutes ago. I don't think she came back in."

Parker pushed through the swinging door into the kitchen and ran for the back door.

He burst through into an alley where a large trash bin stood. There was no sign of Abby.

Parker checked behind the trash bin and ran around the side of the building back to the front, where the emergency medical personnel were loading the old woman into the ambulance with her little white dog.

Still, he couldn't find Abby.

He hurried toward Trace and Matt, who stood with the firefighters.

Trace turned as Parker joined them. "What's wrong?"

"Abby," Parker said. "I can't find her."

Matt turned with Trace and searched the faces of the people standing around the wreck. "When was the last time you saw her?"

"Right before we ran out of the diner."

"Have you checked inside?" Matt asked.

"She's not in the diner. One of the waitresses said she went out through the kitchen trying to catch up with the waitress named Misty before she left with her deputy boyfriend."

Trace frowned. "Did she tell you she was going to talk to Misty?"

Parker shook his head. "I thought she was right behind me when we came out. Then the dog. Now she's gone."

"Why would she try to catch Misty before she left?"

Parker shook his head, thinking back to their conversations with the waitress. Then he remembered. "Misty was ending her shift. Her boyfriend, Deputy Tackett, mentioned he was going to Mexico. Misty was going with him." He smacked his forehead and shook his head. "He said he had a friend who was going to fly him down."

Matt nodded. "And right now, you're thinking Brandon Marshall is the friend."

"Think about it. It makes sense," Parker said. "Marshall knows the places to hide the women and he has a plane to transport them. The runaway teen and the girl walking home from her bus stop both said the man who abducted them was nice-looking, open, friendly and trustworthy, with light-colored hair and blue-gray eyes. Like Deputy Tackett," Parker said. "Abby might have come to that conclusion and was going to warn Misty."

"We don't know that for certain," Trace said.

"Do we know where Marshall keeps his plane?" Matt asked.

"We have a small general aviation airport just outside of town with a 3600-foot runway," Trace said. "He might take off from there."

"Are there private hangars out there?" Parker asked, his pulse picking up.

"Yes," Matt said. "A perfect place to hide women and stage them for a flight to Mexico."

The three men moved at the same time, racing for their vehicles.

"I'll tell Levi and Becker to meet us out at the airport."

"What about the sheriff's department?" Matt asked.

Trace shook his head. "We don't know if Deputy Tackett carries a police scanner. If we alert the department, he'll know and could warn the others. I'll let Levi know to pass the information to Dallas without going through 911 dispatch."

"We need to hurry," Parker said. "Tackett was heading to Mexico this afternoon, as soon as he collected Misty."

"Why would he take his girlfriend with a transport of captives?" Matt asked. "I would think he wouldn't want her to know what he was up to."

"Unless he was only leading her on with the intention of adding her to the collection of women they intend to sell." Parker swung up into his truck, started the engine and zigzagged past the emergency vehicles and out onto Main Street. He followed Trace's truck as the man flew through town.

It would only take ten minutes to get to the airport.

Parker prayed they wouldn't be too late to stop them.

ABBY FOUGHT AND won her effort to stay awake and not succumb to unconsciousness. She pushed and shoved Misty over to lie next to her in the trunk. She felt for a pulse, happy to find a strong one. It worried her that the woman had yet to wake.

As Abby lay in the dark, she tried to think, to come up with a plan to get herself and now Misty out of the back of Sonny's trunk. She had to let Parker and Trace know who was behind the abductions before the women were flown to Mexico in Brandon Marshall's plane.

She'd been right to suspect the handsome deputy. He had to have been the man who'd lured the teens.

His face looked completely innocent. A man a girl could trust.

Her mind flashed back to the men who'd been at the house when she'd tried to escape out the back door.

It made sense that their jailer was Roy Felton. Not many men were six feet four inches tall.

As for the man she'd run into when she'd tried to escape from the house through the kitchen door, she recalled he was a big guy with broad shoulders. Like a man who could've been a defensive lineman on a football team. The temporary tag was an important clue. William Dutton had been there that night.

Then there was the man in the white mask, wearing a tailored suit. She'd been intent on escape but was almost positive she'd seen a flash of silver hair. And he'd hurt his hand when she'd knocked him over.

At the real estate office, Brandon Marshall had winced when he shook hands with Parker. The pieces were all there. These were the men who'd kidnapped her and the others.

The good thing about being captured again was that the deputy would take her to where they were keeping the others. She'd escaped once; she could do it again. This time, she'd take the others with her.

Misty stirred and moaned.

"Hey," Abby touched her shoulder. "Misty, wake up."

"What? Where?" She tried to sit up and bumped

her head against the trunk lid. "What happened? Where are we?"

"Your boyfriend put us in the trunk. I suspect he's taking us to the airport to fly us to Mexico." Abby snorted. "And not for an all-inclusive vacation at a resort. Most likely we'll be delivered to a buyer."

"I don't understand," Misty said. "Why would Sonny do this?"

"Human trafficking is serious business and very lucrative," Abby said. "He's got this fancy car which I'm sure he couldn't afford on his deputy salary."

"He said he bought it used from his uncle," Misty said.

"Smells new to me," Abby said.

"He's going to sell us? But he's my boyfriend. I thought he loved me." She ended with a sob. "Human trafficking... Is that like the sex trade?"

"Yes," Abby said. "But it's not going to happen to us. We're going to get out of this."

Misty stopped sniffling and asked, "How?"

"I don't know. Feel around the inside of this trunk. Is there a release handle to open the lid from the inside? Also, if we can't find a way to get out, we have to be ready to make an escape when the lid is opened. Feel around for anything that can be used as a weapon."

"Okay," Misty said, her tone firming. The waitress wouldn't sit back and accept her fate; she was willing to fight to be free.

"There should be tire tools in here somewhere," Abby said.

"I think I'm lying on the compartment opening," Misty said. She scooted toward Abby and managed to lift the cover over the tools needed to change a tire.

Abby reached over Misty and felt the different shapes, picturing them in her mind. By feeling each tool, she was able to identify them, and her hand finally closed around a tire iron.

"What are you going to do with it?" Misty asked.

"I'm going to use it to fight my way out of here."

"Is there another?"

Abby weighed the tool in her hands. "There's usually only one in each vehicle."

"You should let me have it," Misty said, her voice hard. "I owe Sonny for almost choking me to death."

"He'll pay for his part in what these men have done."

The car slowed and turned, coming to a stop.

"Be ready," Abby whispered. She slid the tool beneath her shirt behind her.

"For what?" she asked.

"Anything," Abby said. "Mostly, be ready to run."

The driver's door opened and closed a moment later.

Abby held her breath, straining to hear footsteps approaching the trunk. She waited, the tire iron hidden beneath her.

Misty would get out first. Once she was on her feet, Abby would follow and whack Sonny in the head like he'd hit her. Hopefully, it would knock him out and they could make their escape.

Seconds went by, then minutes.

"Did he just leave us here?" Misty asked, keeping her voice quiet. "I should have known he was too good to be true."

"He had a lot of people fooled," Abby said. "He's been working with some other men in this operation. I just hope he's still alone when he opens the trunk."

"How did I not see this?" Misty said. "He talked about going to Mexico. I had no idea he was trafficking women."

"We need to put the men responsible for this travesty into prison for a very long time. But we can't do that unless we find a way out." Abby scooted around until her head rested on Misty's leg. "I hope you don't mind. It's tight in here.

"Don't worry about it," Misty said. "Tell me what you want me to do."

"Just stay where you are for now," Abby said. "I want to see if I can fold the seats down." She planted her feet on the backs of the seats and pushed hard.

The seats didn't budge.

Cocking her legs, she kicked out as hard as she could. The seats held firm.

"Shh," Misty said. "I hear someone coming."

Abby scooted back into position and lay next to Misty. She wrapped her fingers around the tire iron that rested against her hip and thigh inside the leg of her jeans. She bunched her muscles, ready to fly out of the trunk as soon as an opportunity presented itself.

Voices sounded along with the footsteps, though they were too muffled to hear clearly.

A moment later, the trunk lid opened.

Abby looked around to get her bearings and look for an escape route. They were inside an aircraft hangar. A plane stood nearby with the steps lowered.

Her pulse quickened. This was it. They were preparing to take them to Mexico if Sonny's claim could be believed. He'd said he had a friend who would fly him there.

Sonny stood in front of the trunk with another man. The other man wore the white mask he'd worn at the Golenski house. When he turned, Abby could see the silver hair and the tailored suit she'd seen Brandon Marshall wearing earlier. Beyond the two men was the wide-open door with bright Texas sunshine streaming through.

All Abby had to do was get past the doors.

Then again, she couldn't make her break until she located the other women. She could not leave them behind again.

She wished she had a tire iron for each of them. It would help give them more of a fighting chance against the two large men.

Another vehicle pulled into the hangar and a man got out, pulling a ski mask into place over his head. The broad shoulders and the shiny new car gave this one away. William Dutton had arrived.

"Get them on the plane," Marshall said. "We leave as soon as we're all on board. Good job getting our quota."

Sonny glanced into the trunk with no expression on his face. The nice guy smile was gone. The blue-gray eyes were more of a hard, steely gray. "Get out," he ordered.

"Sonny," Misty said. "Why are you doing this? Take me back home. I don't want to go to Mexico with you anymore."

"The choice is not yours." His voice was cold, unbending. "Now, get out. Both of you."

Misty climbed out of the trunk and stood in front of Sonny. "What you're doing is wrong," she said. "You don't have to go through with this."

Abby scooted toward the opening, careful to keep the tire iron out of sight as she moved. With the tire iron tucked into her back waistband and hidden beneath her shirt, she eased over the rim of the trunk and out onto her feet. When she straightened, she kept her back turned away from the men.

If they looked at her back, they would know something wasn't right.

"Move," Sonny ordered and shoved Misty toward the plane.

"Sonny, what's wrong with you?" Misty asked. "You're not like this. You're a good man. An officer of the law, sworn to protect."

The man in the white mask snorted. "Morals and

integrity pale in comparison to cold, hard cash. Don't they, Sonny?"

The deputy's lip curled. "Especially when there's a lot of it."

"We're wasting time," Marshall said. "Get them on the plane with the others and drug them. I don't want any more slipups."

A tall figure appeared at the top of the stairs of the airplane.

"Roy, help get our last two guests on board. You know what to do." Marshall left Sonny and Roy to do the job and walked over to where Dutton was grabbing a suitcase from the trunk of his vehicle.

Abby knew she couldn't fight off four men with one tire iron. And from the bulge beneath Marshall's jacket, he was obviously armed.

Sonny had his gun out where she could see it. He turned to her and gave her a narrow-eyed glare. "Give me any trouble and I'll do to you what I did to her. Now, move."

If she wanted to get away, it had to be now, before Roy closed the distance between them. The trouble was that the other women were on board that aircraft. If the plane left the ground, there would be no going back.

Abby had to make sure that didn't happen. The tire iron would come in handy if she could manage to get into the cockpit and damage the controls and ground the plane. Then she could use the tire iron on the men.

She walked between Sonny and Misty toward the plane.

Roy came down to the bottom of the steps, grabbed Misty's arm and dragged her to the top. She looked over her shoulder at Abby before Roy pulled her inside.

Abby started up the stairs, trying to look normal when the tire iron was slipping lower.

"Move a little faster. We don't have all day," Sonny started to shove her from behind.

She turned to keep him from touching the metal, stumbled backward against the steps and the tire iron made a clunking sound.

Abby's heart skipped several beats. She coughed in an attempt to mask the sound and kept moving. When she reached the top of the stairs, Sonny shoved her again, sending her staggering into the plane.

What she saw made her gasp. Cara Jo, Rachel, Laura and Valentina were strapped to the plush leather seats, out cold. Roy held some kind of medical vial with a syringe stuck inside it. He pulled the plunger and drained the vial into the syringe and tossed the empty vial into a cup holder.

When he reached for Misty, she backed away.

"No," she said. "I won't fight you. Just don't drug me. Please."

Roy grabbed her arm and jammed the needle into her arm, injecting half of the liquid into her.

"Please, noooo." Misty slumped.

Roy, still holding onto her arm, eased her into a

chair and turned toward Abby with the remainder of whatever evil was in the syringe.

It was now or never. Abby spun and shoved Sonny backward as hard as she could. He teetered on the top step, reached for her arm, missed and fell backward down the stairs.

Abby yanked the tire iron from her waistband and swung it at Roy's hand carrying the syringe. The loud crack of metal hitting bone preceded the launch of the syringe across the cabin. It crashed into a window and dropped to the floor.

Abby turned toward the cockpit and dove for the controls.

She only made it one step through the door before she was grabbed by her hair and yanked backward into Roy's chest.

With both hands, she raised the tire iron over the top of her head and slammed it into Roy's head. When she cocked her arms to do it again, Roy grabbed the tire iron on her upswing and grabbed it from her grip. Then he pulled her arms behind her and secured her wrists with a zip tie.

By that time, Sonny had made his way back up the stairs, his face a mottled red, an angry bruise on his cheek. He raised his arm across his chest.

Abby cringed, waiting for him to backhand her into the next county.

"Don't!" Brandon Marshall's booming voice arrested Sonny's hand in midmotion. "Don't damage the goods. Our customers pay top dollar if they're in good physical condition." He climbed the steps behind Sonny.

The deputy remained stiff in the doorway for another long moment.

"Save it," Marshall said, stepping past Sonny. "We need to leave before anyone figures out what's going on. You realize, we probably won't be coming back."

Sonny finally moved out of the doorway, his glare on Abby. "Being a deputy for barely more than minimum wage isn't worth putting on the uniform. After we're paid, I'm going to find me a little casita on the beach. There's nothing to keep me here."

"Or me." William Dutton entered the plane, pulling off the ski mask as he settled into one of the seats. "I'm tired of selling cars, barely making enough to pay salaries, commissions and overhead. I'm with Sonny. A casita on a beach is where I'm headed."

Roy grabbed Abby's arms and marched her to one of the chairs near the other women and forced her to sit.

"You won't get away with this. What you're doing is horribly wrong. How can you sleep at night?"

"Like a baby," Marshall said. He looked back at Roy. "Drug her."

Roy reached for the syringe that had flown across the cabin. He held it up and frowned. The syringe was empty, and the needle was bent. "That was the last of the drug," he said.

"Then can you at least slap some duct tape over her mouth?" Marshall said. "I don't want to hear a sound on this flight. But first, close the hatch. We need to get into the air."

. He moved forward into the cockpit, settled into the pilot's seat and fired up the engines.

"Ain't got no duct tape," Roy muttered. He zip-tied her wrists to the armrests. "Start flappin' your gums and I'll use that tire iron on you in spite of what the boss says."

As the plane taxied out away from the hangar, Abby's heart hit the bottom of her belly. This was it. She'd failed to stop these men from ruining the lives of six women. When the plane left the ground, there wouldn't be a cavalry swooping in to save the day. They'd be sold into sex slavery, used and abused in some hovel. Maybe she'd get used to the drugs if they dulled the pain.

She wished she'd had a chance to get to know Parker better. She really liked him and there was a good chance she loved him.

Chapter Fourteen

Trace reached the turnoff to the Whiskey Gulch Municipal Airport and skidded around the corner, barely having slowed enough to make the turn.

Parker repeated the maneuver riding close on Trace's tail. He shot a glance at the runway, his heart in his throat, wondering if they were too late. He'd managed to open the flight app for Marshall's plane's tail number. The man had filed a flight plan from Whiskey Gulch to Monterrey, Mexico, scheduled to leave a few minutes ago.

They couldn't be too late. Abby would be on that plane. Parker wasn't ready or willing to end their relationship. It had only just begun, and he wanted many more years with her. He'd even admit to love at first sight and take a helluva lot of ribbing from the other members of the team. He didn't care as long as he had Abby.

While Trace headed for the gate, Parker rode along the fence paralleling the runway, searching for any sign of a plane. His breath held, and despair sank into every fiber of his being.

A flash of reflected light captured his attention. At the very end of the taxiway, a plane turned and started down the runway, picking up speed.

"No," Parker yelled. "You're not taking her." He yanked his steering wheel to the right and rammed his truck through the chain-link fence, bumped down into a ditch and back up onto the concrete runway, racing toward the plane coming straight at him.

Trace smashed through the gate and raced to catch up to the plane.

Parker wasn't sure how he could stop a plane with his truck, but he had to do something. They could not leave the ground.

He had to reach the plane before it reached its takeoff speed. Not knowing how fast or soon that would be, he just had to get to the plane as quickly as he could.

Sixty…seventy…eighty miles per hour, he pushed the truck faster.

The plane sped down the runway without slowing.

Parker had to make a decision and fast. Did he play chicken and risk crashing into the aircraft, or did he dodge around it and watch it go airborne with Abby and five other women aboard? They'd be alive but disappear into a dark abyss of drugs, sex and abuse.

Parker's jaw set with determination. He would not let that plane leave the ground.

As he neared the point of no return, he slammed on his brakes and turned sideways across the runway, the truck's forward momentum sending him skidding ever closer to the aircraft.

He raised his arms to shield his face for the collision.

At the last moment, the pilot turned off the runway, down into a shallow ditch. Still going too fast to come to a complete halt, it rammed through the airport fence and rolled to a stop in a hayfield.

Parker raced after the plane with Trace not far behind.

Skidding to a halt twenty yards from the tail, Parker shifted into Park, grabbed the AR15 from the back seat and leaped down from his truck. He used the door for cover as he aimed at the top of the stairs ready to shoot.

The aircraft stairs were lowered. For a long moment, nothing happened. No one emerged from inside the aircraft, and no one shouted out a list of demands.

Suddenly, Abby appeared at the top of the stairs, her hands secured behind her back, the barrel of a handgun pressed to her temple by Sonny Tackett.

"We want safe passage for this airplane to Mexico, or this woman dies," he shouted.

"If that woman dies," Parker said, "You and your people die with her."

Trace parked several yards from where Parker

stood. He and Matt reached for their rifles, got out and locked in on the deputy.

Sirens wailed in the distance.

"It's over, Sonny," Trace called out. "Release the hostages and your sentence will be lighter. You pay a lot higher price for murder."

"You hear that, Marshall? Dutton?" Trace shouted loud enough for the men inside to hear. "You aren't killers," Trace said. "Don't add murder to your sentence."

Another truck pulled up behind Parker's.

Parker didn't shift his focus for even a second.

"Sonny," Dallas called out. "You know that plane isn't going anywhere."

"That's right, Sonny," Parker added. "There's too much damage."

"Then get us another," Sonny said. "I'm not going down for this."

"You know that isn't possible, Sonny," Dallas said. "There isn't going to be another plane. You're not going to Mexico. You're going to let Abby go and turn yourself in."

"No."

Brandon Marshall stepped up behind the former deputy. "It's over, Tackett. Put down your gun."

"No," Sonny said. "I'm going to Mexico. If we stay here, we go to jail."

"If you go to Mexico, the Mexican government will extradite you," Dallas said.

"They don't want our criminals," Levi said. "They

have enough of their own. You'll be right back here with a heavier sentence."

"If you want to stand here and argue, leave me out of this." Marshall pushed past Sonny and Abby and descended the stairs, raising his hands as he walked toward Dallas.

"Dutton?" Parker called out.

"I'm coming," he said. "Don't shoot."

William Dutton pushed past Sonny and Abby. "Give it up," he said as he passed. "I didn't sign up for murder. Neither did you." Dutton descended the stairs and hurried toward the trucks, his hand held high.

Roy Felton appeared next. "I didn't sign up for murder, either. Take me to jail. It's easier than finding a job with a rap sheet hanging around your neck." He slipped by Sonny and hurried down the steps and marched up to Dallas with his hands held out, ready for her to cuff him. She pulled his hands behind his back and secured them with zip ties. Then she had him, Marshall and Dutton sit in the grass until transport arrived.

"That leaves you, Sonny," Trace said. "Let her go and give yourself up."

"No." Sonny shook his head. "I want that plane. If I don't get it, I start shooting, starting with her. And I have five more to choose from. So, what's it to be?"

"We can't get you a plane," Trace said. "Put down your weapon before someone gets hurt."

"You're not listening," Sonny said. "Maybe you

will when I start shooting. I'll give to the count of three to get on your phone and call in favors from your rich friends. One…"

Parker looked down his scope, setting the crosshairs across Sonny's face, just above Abby's head. If he took the shot, he could miss and hit Abby instead. If he didn't take the shot, Sonny would. At point-blank, he wouldn't miss.

"Two…" Sonny shouted.

Abby threw herself off the stairs.

Sonny aimed at her falling figure.

Parker took the shot, hitting Sonny square in the heart.

The deputy's knees buckled, and he tumbled down the stairs and lay at the bottom.

Parker, Levi, Trace and Matt rushed forward.

Parker knelt beside Abby and helped her to a sitting position. He pulled his pocketknife out and cut the zip tie. Then he gathered her in his arms and held her. She circled her arms around his neck and clung to him, her body shaking so hard her teeth chattered.

When the trembling subsided, she said, "I n-need to see the others."

A fire engine and three ambulances arrived.

He smiled and brushed a strand of her hair out of her face. "Let the professionals get them out of the plane first."

She nodded and leaned into him. "Just when I thought all was lost, the cavalry came through. Thank you."

"I died a thousand deaths between the time I realized you were gone and now." He pressed his forehead against hers.

She looked up and stared into his eyes. "How did you keep the plane from taking off?"

He drew in a breath and let it out. "You know those thousand deaths I was telling you about? That was 999 of them."

Trace laid a hand on Parker's shoulder. "He took a calculated risk and it paid off."

Matt stepped up behind Parker. "I've never seen a truck play chicken with an airplane."

Abby frowned. "Chicken?"

Parker pushed to his feet. "Let's get the medics to look you over after your spectacular fall. Then we can go back to the ranch and get some rest."

"I'll want to visit the hospital," she said as he helped her to her feet.

"We can make that happen," he said. He scooped her up into his arms and carried her to one of the ambulances for a quick once-over by an EMT.

By the time he declared her okay, the firefighters started bringing the other women out of the plane, one at a time.

Still heavily sedated, they slept through it all.

"Will they be all right?" Abby asked.

Trace nodded. "I spoke with one of the emergency medical technicians. He said the drugs should wear off in a couple hours. They're going to be okay."

"See?" Parker swung her up into his arms. "You kept your promise and brought help."

She shook her head. "The real heroes are you, the Outriders and Dallas."

"We wouldn't have known of their existence if you hadn't risked your life breaking out of the house and running through a thunderstorm to get help."

She wrapped her arm around his neck and smiled. "Oh, and don't forget the hogs."

He chuckled. "I'll never forget the hogs."

"And Brutus is a hero for saving me from them."

"And we won't forget Brutus's bravery." He settled her into the front seat of his pickup, leaned over and brushed a kiss across her lips and said, "When our grandchildren ask me if I think it was worth it to play chicken with an airplane, I'll tell them hell yeah. But I won't recommend they try it."

Epilogue

Two months later

"Thank you for letting us have his reunion here at the Whiskey Gulch Ranch," Abby said. "I was going to have it at our cottage in town, but it just wasn't big enough for all the Outriders, their gals, my fellow abductees and their families."

Rosalyn and Trace stood beside Abby on the porch looking out at the lawn, where Levi, Dallas, Matt and Aubrey were playing a rousing game of volleyball against Irish, Tessa, Becker and Olivia.

Laura Owens sat with Cara Jo Noble and Valentina Ramirez, giving them advice on how to prepare for college. She'd taken the teens under her wing and encouraged them to reach for the stars. She'd spent hours on the phone with Cara Jo, convincing her to get her GED and go on to a junior college to get her core courses and build her grade point average before applying to a four-year institution.

Valentina's mother sat with Rachel Pratt and her two small children on a blanket in the grass.

Rosalyn hugged Abby. "I want to thank you for getting married so quickly to our handsome Parker."

Abby's brow wrinkled. "Why?"

She grinned and looked up at her son. "Because you two committed so quickly, it reminded Trace and Lily that they had yet to set a date for their wedding."

Lily joined them on the porch. "We've decided to get married next month," she said, beaming up at Trace.

"It's going to be a challenge to make it happen so quickly," Rosalyn said. "But we will make it happen."

"We have to." Lily wrapped her arm around Trace's waist. "We can't wait any longer or I won't fit into a wedding dress."

Trace frowned down at her. "Why wouldn't you fit into a wedding dress?"

Lily pulled a white plastic stick out of her pocket and grinned.

Trace's eyes widened. "Are you?"

Lily nodded. "I am."

He grabbed her up and swung her around and then kissed her soundly. "We're going to have a baby," he shouted.

The volleyball game paused long enough for everyone to congratulate the couple.

Abby couldn't have been happier for Lily and

Trace. She smiled at the glow in Lily's cheeks and sighed.

Parker slipped up behind her and pulled her against him. "You look happy."

Her smile broadened. "I am."

"You're not too sad about leaving your old school behind to move up to Whiskey Gulch?"

She shook her head. "Not at all. I'm happy to be with you and surrounded by all the members of your team. We have such wonderful friends who are more like family, and a lovely cottage just the right size for a growing family."

He cupped his hands over her still-flat belly. "Why didn't you say something when Trace and Lily made their announcement?"

She laid her hands over his. "They deserve the spotlight. They brought us all together and made this team a family. I'm just happy to know our child will have friends to play with. We are truly blessed."

"Yes, we are," Parker said. "I love you, Mrs. Shaw."

A wet nose bumped against Abby's leg. She reached down and scratched behind Brutus's ear. "I love you, Mr. Shaw, and Brutus, and Jasper."

* * * * *

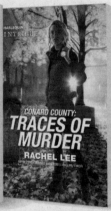

COMING NEXT MONTH FROM

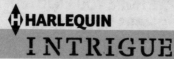

HARLEQUIN
INTRIGUE

#2103 CONARD COUNTY: CHRISTMAS CRIME SPREE
Conard County: The Next Generation • by Rachel Lee
Savage attacks on several women in parson Molly Canton's parish threaten the holiday season. Assisting Detective Callum McCloud's investigation, Molly is drawn to the tortured man. But once the detective realizes these attacks are a smoke screen obscuring the real target—Molly—the stakes escalate...especially now that Molly's goodness has breached Callum's calloused heart.

#2104 POLICE DOG PROCEDURAL
K-9s on Patrol • by Lena Diaz
When police lieutenant Macon Ridley and his K-9, Bogie, respond to a call from Daniels Canine Academy, they discover a baby on DCA's doorstep. Even more surprising, the chemistry that sizzled when Macon first met Emma Daniels sparks once again. Now, not only is an innocent infant's life at stake but so is Emma's...

#2105 EAGLE MOUNTAIN CLIFFHANGER
Eagle Mountain Search and Rescue • by Cindi Myers
Responding to the reports of a car accident, newcomer Deputy Jake Gwynn finds a murder scene instead. Search and rescue paramedic Hannah Richards tried to care for the likely suspect before he slipped away—and now he's gone from injured man to serial killer on the loose. And she's his next target.

#2106 SMALL TOWN VANISHING
Covert Cowboy Soldiers • by Nicole Helm
Rancher Brody Thompson's got a knack for finding things, even in the wild and remote Wyoming landscape he's just begun to call home. So when Kate Phillips asks for Brody's help in solving her father's decade-old disappearance, he's intrigued. But there's a steep price to pay for uncovering the truth...

#2107 PRESUMED DEAD
Defenders of Battle Mountain • by Nichole Severn
Forced to partner up, reserve officer Kendric Hudson and missing persons agent Campbell Dwyer work a baffling abduction case that gets more dangerous with each new revelation. As they battle a mounting threat, they must also trust one another with their deepest secrets.

#2108 WYOMING WINTER RESCUE
Cowboy State Lawmen • by Juno Rushdan
Trying to stop a murderous patient has consumed psychotherapist Lynn Delgado. But when a serial killer targets Lynn, she must accept protection and turn to lawman Nash Garner for help. As she flees the killer in a raging blizzard, Nash follows, risking everything to save the woman she's falling for.

HICNM0922

The whole desperate plan began simply as a last-ditch attempt to save his life. He never intended for anyone to get hurt. That day, not long after Thanksgiving, he walked into the bank full of hope. It was the first time he'd ever asked for a loan. It was also the first time he'd ever seen executive loan officer Carla Richmond.

When he tapped at her open doorway, she looked up from that big desk of hers. He thought she was too young and pretty with her big blue eyes and all that curly chestnut-brown hair to make the decision as to whether he lived or died.

She had a great smile as she got to her feet to offer him a seat.

He felt so out of place in her plush office that he stood in the doorway nervously kneading the brim of his worn baseball cap for a moment before stepping in. As he did, her blue-eyed gaze took in his ill-fitting clothing hanging on his rangy body, his bad haircut, his large, weathered hands.

He told himself that she'd already made up her mind before he even sat down. She didn't give men like him a second look—let alone money. Like his father always said, bankers never gave dough to poor people who actually needed it. They just helped their rich friends.

Right away Carla Richmond made him feel small with her questions about his employment record, what he had for collateral, why he needed the money and how he planned to repay it. He'd recently lost one crappy job and was in the process of starting another temporary one, and all he had to show for the years he'd worked hard labor since high school was an old pickup and a pile of bills.

He took the forms she handed him and thanked her, knowing he wasn't going to bother filling them in. On the way out of her office, he balled them up and dropped them in the trash. All the way to his pickup, he mentally kicked himself for being such a fool. What had he expected?

No one was going to give him money, even to save his life—especially some woman in a suit behind a big desk in an air-conditioned office. It didn't matter that she didn't have a clue how desperate he really was. All she'd seen when she'd looked at him was a loser. To think that he'd bought a new pair of jeans with the last of his cash and borrowed a too-large button-up shirt from a former coworker for this meeting.

After climbing into his truck, he sat for a moment, too scared and sick at heart to start the engine. The worst part was the thought of going home and telling Jesse. The way his luck was going, she would walk out on him. Not that he could blame her, since his gambling had gotten them into this mess.

He thought about blowing off work, since his new job was only temporary anyway, and going straight to the bar. Then he reminded himself that he'd spent the last of his money on the jeans. He couldn't even afford a beer. His own fault, he reminded himself. He'd only made things worse when he'd gone to a loan shark for cash and then stupidly gambled the money, thinking he could make back what he owed and then some when he won. He'd been so sure his luck had changed for the better when he'd met Jesse.

Last time the two thugs had come to collect the interest on the loan, they'd left him bleeding in the dirt outside his rented house. They would be back any day.

With a curse, he started the pickup. A cloud of exhaust blew out the back as he headed home to face Jesse with the bad news. Asking for a loan had been a long shot, but still he couldn't help thinking about the disappointment he'd see in her eyes when he told her. They'd planned to go out tonight for an expensive dinner with the loan money to celebrate.

As he drove home, his humiliation began to fester like a sore that just wouldn't heal. Had he known even then how this was going to end? Or was he still telling himself he was just a nice guy who'd made some mistakes, had some bad luck and gotten involved with the wrong people?

Don't miss
Christmas Ransom *by B.J. Daniels,*
available December 2022 wherever
Harlequin books and ebooks are sold.

Harlequin.com

Get 4 FREE REWARDS!

We'll send you 2 FREE Books plus 2 FREE Mystery Gifts.

FREE Value Over **$20**

Both the **Harlequin Intrigue®** and **Harlequin® Romantic Suspense** series feature compelling novels filled with heart-racing action-packed romance that will keep you on the edge of your seat.

HARLEQUIN
PLUS

Announcing a **BRAND-NEW** multimedia subscription service for romance fans like you!

Read, Watch and Play.

Experience the easiest way to get the romance content you crave.

Start your **FREE 7 DAY TRIAL** at <u>www.harlequinplus.com/freetrial</u>.

HARLEQUIN

Heartfelt or thrilling, passionate or uplifting—Harlequin is more than just happily-ever-after.

With twelve different series to choose from and new books available every month, you are sure to find stories that will move you, uplift you, inspire and delight you.

SIGN UP FOR THE HARLEQUIN NEWSLETTER

Be the first to hear about great new reads and exciting offers!

Harlequin.com/newsletters